WISH WINDS

An Inspirational Novel

※ ※ ※

WISH WINDS

An Inspirational Novel

DANIEL HILL ZAFREN

Copyright © 2014 by Daniel Hill Zafren

Published by Time Treasures Books, West Jefferson, North Carolina

ISBN 13: 978-0-9833042-3-4

Printed in the United States of America

Cover and interior design by Susan Newman Design Inc.

Earlier captivating works by this celebrated author are listed below. Each is distinct and presents significant life lessons in an interesting setting with memorable characters.

In a World We Never Made (2001)
A Door Never Opened (2003)
Shadow Selves (2005)
Network of Death (2006)
Not Lost – Just Not Found (2008)
Restless Beauty (2009)
Glimpses of Forgotten Dreams (2010)
Echo in the Heart (2011)
Double Hugs (2011)
Page Passage (2013)

www.timetreasuresbooks.com

The mediocre teacher tells. The good teacher explains. The superior teacher demonstrates. The great teacher inspires.

— William Arthur Ward

There are two kinds of teachers; the kind that fill you with so much quail shot that you can't move, and the kind that just gives you a little prod from behind and you jump to the skies.

— Robert Frost

The great teachers fill you with hope and shower you with a thousand reasons to embrace all aspects of life.

— Pat Conroy

A master can tell you what he expects of you. A teacher, though, awakens your own expectations.

— Patricia Neal

✳ ✳ ✳

ONE

There was no doubt about it. He was so much more than a teacher that to describe him as a legend in his own time would not be an overstatement. As if he was dispensing candy, visions of hope were created and the realization of dreams became a likely result. Guidance was with a ready and steady hand. He was a friend, a confidant, and an idol. The classes were filled with exploration and entertainment, often of a humorous nature. The lessons learned went far beyond the textbooks. Students were inspired to learn and to follow their dreams.

He retired after forty-seven years at Cornwall High School in Glendale Springs, New York. In twenty-three of those years, he received the New York State Teacher of the Year Award. His influence led to lasting relationships with the students, many of whom went on to major involvement in affairs of the nation and the world or rose to great heights in business and other ventures. Many, still enchanted by his teachings and the memories of a time when the value of a question at times was greater than an answer, remained in touch with him through the years. The mailbox was overflowing on a daily basis.

Retirement brought a different kind of decision-making. He and Glinnis, his wife of fifty years, were still in good health, but it was time to relocate from the severe winters to a more hospitable place. The children and their families had come in for the celebration of the golden wedding anniversary. Their two daughters, Hannah and Elizabeth, lived in Palo Alto, just outside of San Francisco, California, with devoted husbands and two children each. Corey, the son, as yet unmarried lived in Austin, Texas, but he was job hunting in San Francisco and planned to relocate to Palo Alto to enjoy the close relationship with his sisters and to be an active uncle. The children would be overjoyed if the parents wound up moving closer to them.

There are times when a series of events can impact lives in unforeseen ways. He was about to read the letter for the third time just to make sure he grasped it all.

The Catherine Handel School for Girls

1600 Bluemont Avenue

Durham, North Carolina

February 8, 1974

Mr. Grant Albright

269 Pickford Pike

Glendale Springs, New York

Dear Mr. Albright:

This letter will confirm the offer made to you during our telephone conversation last week. It was a distinct pleasure speaking with you.

The Catherine Handel School for Girls has been in existence since 1883, and is noted for its academic excellence. At present, the enrollment is 637 students from grades one through twelve. There are twenty-seven faculty members, all female. Our Governing Board has decided that it may be time for a change. The thought is that some male teachers might provide an academic challenge with a greater variety of perspectives. It was decided that on an experimental basis a male teacher be hired for the 1974 academic year, September, 1974 to June, 1975. We would like to coax you out of retirement to be that male teacher as your outstanding reputation and superior credentials make you an ideal person to fill this position. It may well be a crowning achievement for you as well.

The offer is for the academic year at a salary of $45,000. Your moving expenses will also be reimbursed. Durham is becoming a popular area for retirees. It has a temperate climate, three major universities in the triad area for cultural activities, *and the largest and best hospital in North Carolina.*

Please give this offer due consideration and let us know your decision as soon as possible. Contact me if you have any questions or need further clarification.

I remain faithfully,

Charlene Frentworth
Head Dean

Glinnis was always a major partner in any deliberations. Her levelheaded thinking was an invaluable asset. He liked to refer to her as his love confidant. She read the letter several times as well.

They ate dinner at the small table in the kitchen when it was just the two of them. The more formal table in the dinning room was for company. That evening, they knew what the main topic of conversation would be.

"What do you think, mama-bear?"

"I think first and foremost that papa-bear must decide if it is something he can or wants to do."

"Funny in a way, isn't it? Just when I am settling into a period of inertia, I'm asked to be a pioneer."

"Flattering and well-deserved if you ask me."

"I suppose so. Perhaps, it is a case of mind over matter. I have shifted gears and my thoughts run to other avenues than the world of education."

"My dear, it is not as if they are asking you to dig ditches. They are asking you to do what you love doing."

"Do I sense encouragement in those words?"

"No, you sense support. If your choice is to do it, I'll be with you. If you decide to turn it down, you're still stuck with me."

"Don't you mean stuck on you?"

"For sure." A firm hug sealed that statement.

"Do we ask the children for their thoughts?"

"I am sure they would appreciate being asked, but you know

as well as I do that they will say it is totally our decision. That is as it should be. We taught them to make the decisions that affected them on their own."

He stared at the seemingly frail woman across from him. Lines in the chin, cheeks, and forehead did not diminish the beauty of the face that held him spellbound that evening at the college concert when he first saw her. The small frame defied fatigue or defeat. As a mother and wife she was the fountain of strength they all drank from. Soft-spoken but firm of mind, there was not one day that he regretted their marital union. A family bedrock was the image that stayed with him.

Long after the meal, the discussion continued. The mutual decision reached was that they would take an exploratory trip to Durham where he would visit the school and they would tour the city to see if it appealed to them. Then, hopefully a final decision could be made.

TWO

The visit to the school consumed five hours. The first shock was seeing the students dressed alike in the standard uniform – white long-sleeved blouse, plaid skirt, and plain black loafers. Dean Frentworth explained that the uniform concept minimized distractions related to personal appearances and that there was a correlation between uniforms and discipline. Grant was not sure he bought that explanation, but his time for changing the world was long since gone. In his older age he learned to accept things that might have raised his ire at an earlier period in his life prompting a struggle to change what he did not agree with. The students probably thought he was an inspector and was barely noticed. After all, he was no youthful heartthrob that might have stopped them in their tracks.

Reactions from the teachers were mixed. Evidently, they had been briefed about him. He was introduced to them individually. A few appeared to be friendly enough and voiced encouragement. Most were detached and merely satisfied the formality of meeting him without offering any additional comments or extending any friendly gesture. He had seen it a number of times over the years in various organizations that there was an entrenched force that detested any change even if it might be for the best.

The academic facility was much better than what Cornwall High School had offered. Classrooms were spacious and well lit. Hallways were wide and clean and rows of lockers were in near pristine condition. Laboratories and the gymnasium appeared to be furnished with the latest equipment. The library was well kept and seemed fully adequate for the student population. The cafeteria smelled from disinfectant and not a chair was out-of-place. He was duly impressed, and a school environment, no matter the overtones, was like an old friend.

There did not seem to be any major negative to turn down the offer. The detailed observations were conveyed to Glinnis when he returned to the motel where they were staying.

They drove around Durham as best they could navigate around an unfamiliar place. It was a bit confusing, although it was obviously a college town. Young people were a constant presence in the streets and restaurants and stores appeared geared to that age group. One of the observations he had made over time was that the younger the population the more pizza parlors there were. They passed several retirement villages as they were advertised and from all appearances they were appealing. Not many folks were about and Grant surmised they were taking a nap since he could use one by now.

On the drive home they were mostly silent. It had been pretty much decided to go ahead with the offer, and they had even called a real estate agent before they left Durham to set a date to come back down to look at some houses. They debated about renting a place but it just made better economic sense to purchase a home even if it turned out to be for the short term.

Glinnis stared at his finely etched profile. This feature was not diminished now that the black hair had turned silver. The apt description she had read at some earlier time came to mind about hair color turning silver as the effect of snow on the mountaintop. That profile was the first thing she had noticed about him when she saw him at the college concert. Her wish at the time that he would approach her and introduce himself came true when he talked to her at the gathering in the lobby after the concert. It became a storybook romance. College sweethearts evolved into life long friends and lovers. So many of their friends had suffered through bad marriages and wallowed in discontented lives. She was one of the lucky ones. Finding and holding on to a genuinely good man is a glorious achievement. It is one of life's magical gifts. Each day with this intellectual, considerate, and loving man was a blessing. Throw into the mix three good children and her life was full and its own reward. The prospect of a new chapter in their life was in a way exciting, and she would look forward to the developments as they unfurled. She had learned long ago that everything was better when they experienced it together. Every once and awhile she would shudder thinking about what it might be like without him. Without a doubt, there would be very little. Even though she had tried over the years to get involved in various business ventures after the children were grown, the true significance of her life was and would always be the marriage. She could only hope that if they did not die together she would go first.

Once the offer was formally accepted, things moved quickly. On the second house-hunting trip they found a small ranch home two miles from the school in a quiet neighborhood. They had rejected the choice of a retirement village as the houses were too close together. The house they chose already had an extensive garden and that pleased Glinnis as she had always enjoyed flowers and puttering in a garden. Shopping was close by and it was a reasonable distance from the hospital. The offer on the house was accepted and in early July they moved. The house in Glendale Springs sold quickly, the buyer entranced by the beautiful garden that Glinnis had tended to over the years. They figured that would give them two months to get fully settled before the teaching chore would commence. However, a series of meetings scheduled before the classes started would consume two weeks before the first day of classes.

Surrounded by their furnishings, it did not take long to feel at ease. They explored Durham, including trying some of the restaurants. On the Duke University campus, through a copy of the college newspaper they were pleased by cultural choices offered by the community. They sent in for season tickets to both the college orchestra and the Theater Department productions. Since they had first met at a concert, concerts always were a special attraction. Drama actions also held a special meaning as they both had played in minor parts or helped behind the scenes at their college plays.

The first school meeting was an orientation briefing. There were also two new female teachers, both young and fresh out of teacher's college. Licenses were not required for teaching at private schools. Melanie Baker was from Durham while Elaine Halpern was from Georgia. Both were sincerely glad to meet him and there were indications that the bond as new arrivals would present a closeness. In a way, they had to go up against the old guard as well. The three of them met each member of the Governing Board and the welcoming speeches were long and repetitious. More than once he was singled out as representing a bold step for the school. He was not concerned about living up to something. He had always been his own person and would be steadfast in that role. That worked just fine for forty-seven years at teaching so there was no need to alter it now.

At one of the later meetings, he was informed that he would have a homeroom as well as four Civics classes, a twelfth and seventh grades in the morning and a tenth and fourth grades in the afternoon. The teachers had their own lunchroom, but were on a rotating schedule to police the cafeteria. Civics was generally described as a mixture of history, government, philosophy, and current events. It represented enough of a broad latitude for him to adapt his usual teachings to the groups involved. The greatest challenge might be the fourth grade, as he had never had students that young.

He also found out that many of the teachers were strongly opposed to his addition to the faculty. Some parents were also adamant in a negative reaction when informed of his presence. Any male at the school represented a contrary principle for them as they sent their daughters to this school to be completely removed from any male presence and influence. He supposed he was out on a limb along with the school officials and it might prove to be a shaky one. More may be resting on his presence than meets the eye. Of course, to his way of thinking any influence he might exert was completely blown out of proportion.

On a visit to the library, he detected a possible ally in the librarian, Chance Fleming. She was probably the oldest person at the school besides himself, and old age prompts a kindred spirit. Her lively mannerism belied her years, and he was much impressed by her intellect and knowledge of the library collections. Her name while different was easily explainable. When born, her father was so discouraged since he had wanted a boy that in defiance he named her Chance just on the chance that through his ranting she would turn into a boy.

While Grant was at the meetings, Glinnis investigated prospects for voluntary work to get involved in the community just as she had done in Glendale Springs. Fruitful pickings were available at Duke University. The University Library welcomed her warmly when she offered to help with the collections a day a week. At the hospital, there was a volunteer group to help with the patients. That would be another day a week. For now, the rest of the week would probably be consumed with tending to the house and garden, running errands, and other chores. The weekends would be committed to Grant and their precious time together.

A nearby neighbor brought over a cake to welcome them to the neighborhood. That was a very nice gesture and it bode well for their choice of living space. The wife invited Glinnis to go on a shopping trip so she could show her some of the best places. Glinnis got along well with everyone. Being friendly and easygoing is a magnet to those who appreciate those qualities. Wilma and Benny Braxton had been in the same house their entire married life. They were about twenty years younger than the Albrights, Benny was working at the dairy plant. Wilma would seem to be a good friend in the making. She stayed at home with two sons who were now in high school. She thought she was needed more at home than anywhere else. Glinnis did the same thing when her children were growing up. She and Grant agreed that monitoring and being a constant role model was vital to the well being of a family. It has never been easy to grow up, and it probably never will be.

* * *

THREE

Until Grant's appointment, Chance Fleming had been the oldest person at The Catherine Handel School for Girls. She still clung to the distinction of being at the school longer than anyone else. She had been the Librarian for forty-one years. At the age of sixty-eight, the thought of retiring had crossed her mind with increasing frequency. Yet, it was not the school itself or the students that held her there. It certainly was not the meager salary which she had been barely able to sustain herself with, and savings were probably insufficient to ever let her keep up with the barebones life style she had. Any social security payments would add little help. It was her love for books and the pride she had in keeping the collections orderly and accessible that held her daily attachment to the school. Every once and awhile she might instill the joy of reading in one of the girls and that was a moment to relish and remember.

She liked the fact that a male teacher would be at the school, and she sensed immediately in him a bond not only of age but also by his questions and comments that he had a love for books. There was only a surface acquaintance with the other teachers, and she had no close friends. Other than Frieda Burns who she had grown up with and was close to before that family moved to California before high school, there had been no person to confide in or to share intimate feelings and details of dreams. After all of the years at the school, finally there was a person she wanted to know better. The years had been drab if not downright boring. This year might be different.

It was the Friday before the school year was to start on Monday.

Chance engaged in one of her favorite activities that she looked forward to each year. She would visit each of the teacher's homerooms to see how they were decorated for the entering students. It was a kind of contest among the teachers, and the decorating seemed to be more elaborate each year. The teachers stayed in the homeroom for the entire teaching day as the students moved from class to class.

When she opened the door to Grant's room, she was taken aback. He was sitting at the teacher's desk at the front of the room scribbling on a piece of paper. There was not a single decoration in the room. The walls were blank and the blackboard empty. The only standard item in the room besides the teacher's desk and the rows of student seats was the American flag in a stand in a corner.

Trying to keep the surprise to herself, she quipped, "You had better get started filling up the place or they'll demote you."

He glanced up over his glasses. "Fat chance of that. I'm already at the bottom. I have always let the students decorate as we go along. It seems to have more meaning to them that way, and it sure is easier on me. Besides, if I decorate with certain themes or subjects, it almost commits me to that course. I much rather leave everything open-ended."

"Gee, I never thought of it that way. Sure makes sense. What do the higher-uppers think about you not conforming to tradition?"

"I am not sure they know yet. They have taken me for what I am. And, I sure am what I am. I'm too old and crotchety to change."

"What about the saying that you are never too old to be what you were meant to become?"

"Ah, I am in full compliance with that. This is what I am meant to be so I have become it."

"You'll get no argument from me. I am in the same leaky ship. But, you'll find the other teachers do not tolerate a rebel."

"So, dear lady, what kind of warning signs should I be looking for?"

"My dear man, you know yourself that you are entering troubled waters. You will experience varying degrees of danger, some probably with little or no notice. If I get wind of any specific problems, you can count on me to let you know about them."

"I spotted you as an ally right away."

"It may well take more than an ally. You do realize that it is us against them. We are vastly outnumbered and they can wield much pressure."

He smiled. "Those are the kind of odds that I like. If we lose we have a built in excuse."

She patted him on the arm. It was an endearing gesture and he appreciated it. "There'll be no excuses because there will be no losing."

"That's the spirit!"

* * *

Wish Winds

FOUR

Grant should have guessed that he would be a novelty or an oddity. Out of curiosity or perhaps disbelief, for the first day of school a throng of students waited by the front entrance for Mr. Teacher to arrive.

"Wow! So that is what a man looks like!" Grant heard the humorous remark over the din.

He caught fragments of other quips as a play on words as he made his way toward the large oak doors. "A MANipulator! A ComMANder! A He MAN! Watch your MANners! See the new MANager! Is it a MANaquin?"

There were fourteen students in his homeroom class, a cross-section of all ages. They sat silently in their chairs staring at him. It was so quiet the only sound he heard was his own breathing. He let the quietness prevail for a few moments, letting them secretly guess what he was going to do and say. "Yes, what you see before you is not a mirage. I have always been a man, except in my youth when I was a boy. Before I take the attendance, let me tell you about myself and what I believe about homerooms. I have been a teacher for many years. I went into teaching as a way of guiding and helping young people. The greatest asset of our nation is our young people and not enough attention is given to that fact. Yet, it is not easy being a young person. You get conflicting signals and directions from your parents, schools, and society at large. There are many uncertainties and too many questions that go unanswered. I love teaching and love being a teacher. Being a teacher is more than giving you facts and information. It is a system in place to help you in many ways. Teachers need to listen to your concerns, need to give you an answer if one exists based on their experience and genuine interest in your growth. Teachers can learn from their students. We'll be together at the start and end of each day. As time goes by this homeroom can be a place you can ask questions you may not be able to ask elsewhere, and it should represent a special time to begin and end your day. It is and should be different from all of your other classes."

He took the attendance and sent the students off to their first class. Two senior girls stayed back as they were in his first class of seniors.

Hattie Forester and Shelly Phelps were best friends, although they were nothing alike. Hattie had long black hair and was tall and thin. Shelly had close cropped light brown hair and was short and on the plump side. Grant noticed the animated conversation between them as they waited for the other senior girls to arrive. He was perceptive enough to know over the long years being around youngsters when a friendship was genuine. While he could not hear what they were saying, since they glanced in his direction often he surmised they were talking about him. Dare say he would be the major topic of conversation for probably the whole school year.

Eleven other seniors joined Hattie and Shelly in the class. Grant estimated this was about half of the seniors in the school. Their gaze shifted between him and the barren walls. He was sure the absence of decorations was as mysterious to them as he was.

When they were still and a completed seating chart was passed up to him, he cleared his throat and shifted his eyes to each of the young faces. "I am sure you already know I am Mr. Albright, the first and perhaps last male teacher at The Catherine Handel School for Girls. You have had other Civics classes, but this class will be like no other you have had before. You noticed the empty walls. It is not for me to fill them up. You will be doing that over the year according to what you get out of this class, and it will change as often as the seasons. Each item will be a reminder of what you did and, hopefully, each time you look at them it will reinforce what you have learned. It may even prompt new questions as we build upon each addition."

A petite girl with curly brown hair and wire-rimmed glasses in the front row raised her hand. Grant located her on the seating chart. "Yes, Florence, what are you itching to say?" The girls giggled.

In a squeaky voice, Florence spoke alternating her stare between him and the walls, "We've never done anything like that before. Maybe, it is not allowed."

"Well, young lady, that is precisely why I said this class will be unlike any you have had before. And, putting things on the wall is just the tip of the iceberg. I will do the worrying about what is allowed. Which brings me to another change." He could only guess what they might be thinking. He knew they would be taking away things from the class they could only guess at now.

He walked to the back of the room, every head turning in his direction as he traveled. He thought to himself, *I wonder how long being in awe lasts? Perhaps, I better take advantage of it while I can.*

After he moved back to the front of the class, he continued rather enjoying the rapt attention. "Your parents pay for you to be here, a pretty penny I might add. I am also going to pay for you to be here in my class." A unified gasp filled the room. "Maybe not a pretty penny, which is an expression for a good chunk of money, but a penny none-the-less. I have a bowl here filled with pennies. Each one has a different date on it. I will walk around and you reach in and take one out and it is yours to keep. You will research that year on the penny and make a chart on that year in these categories: international; national; sports; entertainment; fashion; and fads. I hope you are writing this down. Put it on construction paper, any color you wish, 16 x 24, put the year on top, and we will hang them on the walls. Use sources in our library, a public library, whatever you might have at home, and even interview people who might remember occurrences for that time. There are no pennies for the years 1940 through 1945 as World War II overshadowed those years. Besides the actual list, be prepared to tell the class in more detail some of the things you may have found most interesting in the year you are assigned, even if not on the list. Making selections may not be easy. Any questions?"

A sea of raised hands pleased him. Lighting a fire brings action and change. The years had been filled with both. Monetary compensation for teachers is notoriously minimal. It is the reward of intellectual captivation and exploration that binds the teacher to the job. There is no greater journey on Earth.

In the teacher's lunchroom, he sat with the other two new teachers, Melanie Baker and Elaine Halpern. The young women were animated in their descriptions of their first real teaching experience. As if to be reassured by the master, they would often interrupt the narration by asking him if what they had done was right. Before they all returned to their rooms, he coached them with the common sense he knew so well with the contact with youngsters. There is no right for every situation, no perfect way to teach. Take a moment to think before reacting to what you might not be totally prepared for. That often brings the best result. Under reacting can be as bad as over-reacting, but relying on instinct and a humane outlook can usually soothe a crisis.

The fourth grade class squealed with delight at the penny selection game. They were not to make a list but to just concentrate on one event for that year. It was fascinating for him to be teaching such youngsters, and he smiled broadly when one of the girls asked him if she could spend the penny on anything she wanted. Just before the end of the class, he emphasized to the youngsters who could not help staring at him that all learning is a game. "It is a game of exploring, going to places and finding out why it is there and what can be done while visiting. It could be an amusement park where the rides are fun or it can be a jigsaw puzzle where you are given one piece to fit in to the total picture. It may take many attempts before it is just right. The more learning the more fun there is to be had as it becomes clear that many of the things learned also can fit together and lead to further learning."

There were three fourth grade students from the class that were also in his homeroom class. They stayed behind for the end-of-day session as the others made their way out. It had been a long day for everyone and it showed in the slow movements and subdued talking by the students.

When all were present, he declared, "I knew you couldn't keep away from me!" The laughter was genuine. "Tomorrow, it will be my turn to not keep away from you." More laughter brought a relaxed end to the day. "Think about this day tonight and look forward to what tomorrow may bring. Each day is a building block for who you are and for who you will become. I am sure you all know what building blocks are and probably played with them at some time. They can be small or large, and they create the tallest and strongest structure when many are used properly. They create a sturdy base or foundation and then reach up from there. Each day is also a stepping-stone on your wonderful trip to adulthood. Stepping stones are rocks that are located to cross a stream to get to the other side without getting wet. They can be small if the stream flow is gentle and large if the flow of the river is strong and they will enable you not to get swept away in the current. Stepping stones are not only a convenience they can be life saving. Each day can also be marked by a wish wind. Wish winds are dreams and hopes that produce a symbolic wind at your back to help push you to wherever you want to go in life and can also blow away any obstacles in your way. A wish wind may be the most important of the three. Building blocks can be helpful in building character and stepping stones can be used to find your path. It is only a wish wind that can start and keep you going to an accomplishment important to you. We will use plenty of building blocks and stepping stones here, but we will concentrate on wish winds. Once discovered, a wish wind will be the most useful throughout your lives. Building blocks, stepping-stones, and wish winds can be found here. See, the room is not as empty as you thought it was." He soaked in the laughter. There is nothing quite like the sound of a child laughing. After all, it is so natural and so human.

* * *

FIVE

Glinnis was preparing meatloaf for dinner. She knew Grant would be tired and hungry as he always was the first day of school. Yet, the stories and observations would pour out, and she imagined that there would be even more he would share with her from this unusual day. She had stories of her own.

In the morning, Glinnis had gone to do voluntary collections work at the Duke University Library. It was a wonderful facility, and once directed to the books she would be tending to she was entranced by the scope of the holdings. She probably did more reading than organizing, but nobody was monitoring her activity. Just the feel of a book in her hands, especially if it had a leather binding, was gratifying. Being surrounded by rows and rows of books gave her a sense of majesty. In another life, she was sure she would have become a librarian. She and Grant had collected old books over the years, and there was great comfort having them on the shelves lining one wall in the living room. The movers had moaned and groaned lifting the twenty-seven cartons of books in the move. She smiled as she recalled the many evenings they had spent reading, classical music serving as a background to such an enjoyable activity.

In the afternoon she had stopped at the store to get the beef fresh for the meatloaf. People were friendly, and she surmised that maybe there was something to the often-heard pronouncement of southern hospitality. Glendale Springs had been friendly as a small town because people more or less knew each other. Here, a stranger seemed to prompt a continuous acknowledgement of presence and purpose. It was a comforting and endearing feature.

As predicted, Grant relayed every event at the school, embellishing them with the humor and wisdom she so loved about him. As she had thought so often, if there ever was a natural born teacher it was Grant. Establishing a connection with youngsters came quickly and easily, and he shared and empathized with their anxieties and accomplishments. He was not the only lucky one. The students were the true beneficiaries of his caring and perception. Most would stop thinking of him as a teacher and consider him a friend. That would enrich their lives for the moment and for all of the years to come. She had seen it so many times to doubt its existence and longevity. Letters and other forms of communication still came from students he had even decades earlier. There must be a good ten scrapbooks filled with articles sent by former students about them as they made inroads into the worlds of business, politics, entertainment, and sports. They were proud of their deeds and prouder still of sharing it with the mentor that propelled them through life. His influence and encouragement paid many dividends. She also knew how much it meant to him. He had said to her many times that his blessings extended far beyond his immediate family to the perpetual congregation of pupils.

Of course, not all was without certain complications. Schools have internal upheavals just as there are office politics in the business world. It is too bad that such was an impediment to a true and steady progress toward worthwhile goals. As Grant spoke of it, this school was no different, and it might be even worse. He told Glinnis of his brief conversation with Chance when he stopped in at the library to alert her to the possible student onslaught from the penny assignments. Chance was a good contact. As she saw it all, three distinct segments of the faculty were emerging. There was a small but adamant group opposed to his presence and his seemingly radical teaching methods. It was bad enough that he had barren walls in his classroom, and he could count on them being vocal and troublesome when, as they would interpret it, he had made attempts to buy or bribe the students. Another group was guardedly in favor of the major step by the school, and they urged withholding any judgments until well in to the school year. The remaining teachers did not care one way or the other just as long as no one bothered them.

After dinner, they read and listened to Mahlers' First Symphony and Dvorak's New World Symphony. They showered and retired for the night early. His nearly instant deep breathing told her he had fallen asleep. She tightened her arm around him more to reassure herself that she had a life-long hold on him. Love, that age-old emotional mystery, had probably revealed more of its inner workings and secrets to them as they traveled life's pathways together. It continues to be a wonderful journey. That alone led her to a peaceful sleep.

* * *

Wish Winds

SIX

It was not the kind of home she really wanted or dreamed of having, but Chance had made a series of compromises throughout her life. The row house was in a mostly blue-collar neighborhood. The thin walls could not diminish sounds from adjoining units, and varying noises from the street were often disturbing. Yet, she could not afford a better place, and the years melted into each other. Even if she was able to move, there just was not the motivation to effectuate such a plan. Without family, friends, and a major involvement other than the library work, she was a lonely person. Lonely people think and brood too much. For old lonely people such a situation is compounded. Knowing what the problem is does not necessarily make a solution any easier. She had long ago stopped feeling sorry for herself, but it did wear her down and she had become overly pessimistic. After all, there was nothing to look forward to. She would retire some day, and then what would become of her? She resolved these wayward thoughts as she always did with the staunch philosophy that held her together. She would take each day one at a time. It would be self-defeating to look too far ahead just as it was fruitless to look backwards although she could not help doing that at times.

Chance had never married, although that was more her fault than the twist of fate. She had two great loves, and she did not respect or fully appreciate those opportunities. In retrospect, she did not treat either of the men fairly.

When she was nineteen, she met Larry Eckworth. He had dropped out of school and was working in the local factory. He worshipped the ground she walked on. He kept bringing her flowers and showered her with constant attention. Her parents kept telling her she could do better, and eventually their influence soured her on him. It was a cruel dismissal, and she knew she had hurt him deeply. To this day it still bothered her when she thought about it. One cannot do better than to accept sincere affection. The source of an abiding love should never be disrespected.

Soon after her fortieth birthday, she had gone to the University bookstore and an author was there signing his new book on aspects of North Carolina history. He was charming and was fully taken with her. He engaged her in close conversation for over an hour and stayed in Durham an extra week to be with her. They were constant companions for that time, and he made it no mystery that he had fallen madly in love with her. Due to the fast moving developments and because of her overly guarded nature, she questioned the genuineness of his feelings. He pleaded with her to go away with him to his home in Charlotte or that he move here to be with her. A nagging disbelief uncontrollably led her to repeatedly discourage him. She cut short his telephone calls and read his torrent of love letters with suspicion. As soon as he was gone from her life, she realized what she had truly lost. A misplaced pride prevented her from recanting, and the last vestige of passion in her life was gone forever.

The one thought that had taken hold and was becoming the crucial sustaining feature of her well being was that she wanted to write a book of fiction. She had actually started it over the summer, not that she had gotten very far into it. The premise was fully developed. It would be about a lonely woman who desperately wanted a friend. She was hung up on the reality of how and where such a friend might materialize. The usual sources, such as a fellow worker, at church, or at a charity activity, appeared unproductive. If it were to occur by an unusual event, a happenstance, it was difficult to focus on something realistic and believable.

At least the situation with Grant was proving to be a distraction.

She would love to pull the rug out from under those overly prim and proper faculty members who thought they knew it all and believed they controlled everything that went on at the school. More than once their influence had led to decisions about the library she did not agree with. Meekly she had always given in believing her life would be easier that way. Yet, it bothered her that she was so submissive. Now, there might be an opportunity for her to regain some sense of rightness and purpose.

✳ ✳ ✳

SEVEN

What a difference a day makes! On the second day of school, there was no throng of students awaiting his arrival. There were just a few students milling around and they barely noticed him.

Responding to the note in his mailbox that Dean Frentworth wanted to see him before he went to his class, he knocked on her office door as her secretary was not around. He entered when she told him to, and a stern look on her face was not a good sign. Her voice was raspy and authoritative. "What is this I hear about you giving the students money?"

After explaining his penny assignment, her voice softened. "Well, one more prime example of things blown out of proportion."

"One never can get quite accustomed to it, can you?"

"No, not really. The situations change but the nature of the beast is always the same. Everything alright?"

"Sure. Children are wondrous creatures. Simple and complex all rolled into one, whether it be in New York or North Carolina."

He left confirming his belief that Dean Frentworth was a good and fair administrator. That made his job easier. It probably did not make her job that way. After all, pleasing one segment often means running afoul of others.

He ducked in at the Library to bid Chance a good morning. She suggested he have lunch with her in the Library as she shunned the lunchroom to keep any association with the troublesome teachers at a minimum. She said the rumors would fly, but she did not mind if it did not bother him. His response was typical. "It would enhance my image if it is known that I am having a private lunch with a beautiful woman."

In the homeroom, it almost seemed as if the class had been together with him for months. The atmosphere was relaxed and the girls chatted away.

He took the attendance. "In the minutes remaining before you go off to conquer another day, I was thinking we could use this time each day to have a discussion on whatever comes along in school life or life outside of school. If nothing crops up, I'll throw out a subject or read something of interest. Unless there is already a topic to talk about, I will read one of Aesop's Fables." An absence of raised hands prompted him to continue. "Not all lessons can be found in the classroom."

THE LION AND THE MOUSE

A mouse happened to run into the mouth of a sleeping lion, who roused himself, caught him, and was just about eating him, when the little fellow begged him to let him go, saying, "If I am saved, I shall be everlastingly grateful." So, with a smile, the lion let him off. It befell him not long after to be saved by the mouse's gratitude, for when he was caught by some hunters and bound by ropes to a tree, the mouse, hearing his roaring groans, came and gnawed the ropes, and set him free, saying, "You laughed at me once, as if you could receive no return from me, but now, you see, it is you who have to be grateful to me."

The story shows that there come sudden changes of affairs, when the most powerful owe everything to the weakest.

Wish Winds

At lunch, Grant pulled out the meatloaf sandwich Glinnis had made for him with leftovers from dinner along with the usual thermos of coffee. He offered to share both with Chance when he saw she only had a muffin and some water. "Kind of you, but this is what I usually have during the day. I'm trying not to gain any weight so that the girls won't make fun of me. It is bad enough they already call me a bw for bookworm. If I gain any more weight they'll call me a cbw, a chubby bookworm."

"I refuse to give up what I like merely because it might produce an unsightly result. Anyway, my lifeguard days at the beach are over. Glinnis and I walk whenever we can."

"Tell me how you met Glinnis."

"We became college sweethearts after meeting at a school concert."

"And your children?"

"We have two married daughters living in California and grandchildren, and an unmarried son living in Texas. Tell me about you."

"There is little worth telling. I have never married, and I now have too confined a life so that I am afraid to disrupt it."

"I advise my students that when change is deemed necessary or right, they have to take a risk. It is the only way to break out of a restrictive life situation."

"Do you think there is an age limit on taking a risk?"

"Not at all. Look at me being here. Glinnis has also taken this risk and it was not by her choice."

"She sounds like a wonderful person."

"She sure is. The two of you should meet." After a thoughtful pause he continued certain that he was posing a good idea. "In fact, why don't I ask her if she would volunteer to work with you here in the library. She is already volunteering one day a week at the University Library and she has always loved books and libraries."

"That sounds awfully good. I have mentioned numerous times

to Dean Frentworth that I could use help and that if any parent showed an interest in volunteering in the library that would be perfectly fine."

Glinnis thought it was a terrific idea, and she proposed shifting her involvements around so she could be with Grant two days a week. That way they would be close and she would be doing what she liked.

At the end of the day, Chance returned home with rare excitement. She could hardly wait to make an entry in her developing notes for proceeding with the book. The friend would materialize in the guise of a volunteer to help in the work situation.

EIGHT

By the next day, Grant did not have to capture the attention of the homeroom class by doing a reading. After taking the attendance, every hand was raised. The concept of a wish wind had reverberated throughout the school. They all wanted to know more about it, especially how it worked, how it gets started, and how to control it. There is power and mystery in introducing something new, something not fully defined or explored. Throughout the years Grant had seen it repeatedly. Put a new vision in front of a young and curious mind and it is a fish attacking succulent bait with gusto. The real magic a teacher can perform is to make what is old appear to be new. After all, a wish wind is nothing more than setting a goal so that mind and body can attain it. The profound saying emblazoned on the ceiling of the Great Hall at The Library of Congress says it succinctly: *They reach too low who reach beneath the stars.*

"I am delighted that the concept of a wish wind has created a spark. We can and will talk about it more. In the few minutes that we have before you go off to your classes let me just tell you how it differs from building blocks and stepping-stones. You can all share the same blocks and stones, but a wish wind is yours alone. It is personal. Everyone can and should have a wish wind, and you can have more than one. The blocks and stones are already in place for you to use. You alone create a wish wind and you alone know when it is done. Does that answer your questions?"

The loud groans and waving hands told him what he already knew. He had only added fuel to the fire as the lack of specifics raised an even greater curiosity.

Each of his classes was more intent on knowing about a wish wind than the prescribed subject matter. He sidestepped further discussion by informing them that time and circumstance would clarify it all.

At lunch, Chance told him that Dean Frentworth had approved Glinnis helping in the library. She could hardly contain herself. "The whole place is wild about your wish wind. I know the other teachers are envious as they rarely stray from lesson plans and embedded concepts. I suppose I am a bit jealous as well. There are no books in the library on wish winds. So, you must tell me all about them."

He smiled and patted her hand. "There is no way to research a wish wind. It is an act and action of self-discovery and self-motivation. The interesting part is that it is not just for youngsters. People of any age can have a wish wind."

"Even a staid and defeated old woman like me?"

"Especially so."

"How do I get it going?"

"You already have by wanting to. If you want a change ahead for yourself just concentrate on what the change will consist of. Then let the wind rise up at your back to ease the way toward that change."

"And, if I don't exactly know what I wish for?"

"Wishes have a way of defining themselves as you proceed."

"I can see why the students are fascinated. I believe you are a magician and that the school will never be the same."

By the next day, enough of the teachers and parents had complained that the male teacher was filling the heads of the students with nonsense that Dean Frentworth wanted to see him. "Here we go again," her mannerism was firm. "Your explanation better be good."

"It may not be good, but it is simple. A wish wind is just a disguised term for allowing the students to believe in themselves. Its premise is that there is a special future out there for them and that they need to think and plan for it. The classroom is not just a place to study the past and focus on the present. A teacher's greatest gift to a student, in my opinion, is to open the eyes to the past, the present, and the future."

"And are there no dangers in leading them to the unknown or to believe there are forces to propel them somewhere that is unrealistic?"

"The future is full of risks, but the way to delineate a future is to develop a goal and strive towards it. The goal is the wish and the striving is the wind. I believe the more a youngster accepts that he or she can work in the direction of full potential, the teacher has been successful. What can be better than that?"

"Do you also believe that a teacher should be a philosopher?"

"Among a host of other capabilities. How else can we serve as role models?"

"This is a tough sell to parents as well as to other teachers entrenched in the older methods of education. There is great comfort in the status quo. For most minds, schools should not infringe on or diminish parental control and influence."

"We should not let most minds dictate what is right."

"Perhaps, but the reality is that most minds pay the bills. They also fund our existence."

"Chalk it up to my being a radical."

"This is only the first week of school. I knew you would be different and I encourage that. A radical I can tolerate. You are the product of a radical idea. On the other hand, I cannot defend a loose canon."

"I am sure the students will decide eventually who or what I am."

"Is that a wish wind?"

"No, just whether I am a fair wind on potentially troubled seas or merely an old wind bag."

✳ ✳ ✳

Wish Winds

NINE

Glinnis was not surprised either by the exuberance of the students or the adverse parental reaction. She had seen it all before. Grant had employed the wish wind scenario at various times, although she was certain that the last time was more than ten years ago. He had used similar concepts with varying descriptive terms, all designed to lead the students to think of themselves in individual terms with the power to define and control their destiny. It usually did not provoke such strong contrary reactions as the ones Grant described, but there had often been some parent who did not like the idea of a teacher usurping the role of a parent.

She went with Grant to the school the next day to meet Chance and to work at the library. The two women hit it off instantly. Glinnis, highly perceptive as to human traits, could tell that Chance was very intelligent and easy-going. For Chance, the overpowering attraction was Glinnis' out-going maturity. The mutual love of books and a common thread of appreciation for the great writers revealed itself throughout the day. There were numerous conversations ranging from the philosophical to personal beliefs and experiences. The illusive friendship that Chance had desperately hoped for seemed facile in its arrival.

Grant joined them for lunch, and he readily ascertained the budding friendship that he had predicted would develop. Glinnis was such a likable and vivacious person that nearly everyone in contact with her fell under her spell. She was one of those special intriguing persons that seemed to be smiling all of the time, and the smile emanated naturally from within.

After Grant left for a class, the two ladies lingered at the table. A comfortable silence engulfed them. Chance then offered her unrestrained opinion. "Grant is an exceptional teacher. It has taken only a few days to establish that."

"Yes, he is. The best part is that even after this long time he loves it as much as the very first day he stood before a class."

"As much as I love this Library, I am frank to admit that I am tired of it."

"Maybe it is time to try something different."

"For the longest time I have wanted to write a book. I actually started it over the summer."

"What is it about?"

Chance hesitated, the fragility of the friendship subject leading to a cautious and general response. "It is a fictionalized account of a woman seeking fulfillment."

"Sounds interesting, almost tailor-made for a wish wind. We have encountered authors over the years, and I must say that most of them found writing to be stressful although rewarding on a personal level."

"Right now, I am still in the early frustration stage. Ideas float by and I seem to have trouble grasping them. Over the years, I have abandoned many projects, and I hope this one does not end up on the pile."

"I think the secret is to not demand too much of yourself. You possess it. Don't let it possess you."

" I might get to that point, but right now I still look on it as a hobby."

"Even a hobby can be a domineering taskmaster."

"I guess danger lurks everywhere."

"You seem like a person who can handle danger."

"I like to think so, but I probably have not been put fully to the test."

"Do you like music?"

"Yes."

"What kind?"

"I suppose the technical term is easy-listening orchestral works."

"Grant and I love classical music, and over the years that has smoothed out some of the bumps in the road and soothed a whole bunch of agitation. Try writing with music in the background as it might add a relaxing feeling to the writing chore."

"Sure can't hurt. I will try it."

"We met in college at a concert. You might say that music joined our hearts and keeps stirring it as we go along."

"Seems to me that you two should collaborate on a book. It would be filled with a whole host of absorbing stories."

Glinnis had a far off look in her eyes. "Anything and everything is a possibility. The problem is that retirement barely settled in when this teaching offer came along. We touched on a whole host of choices of what to do before that. Where to do it might be the most difficult choice. Our children live out West and are trying to persuade us to move out there to be close to them and the grandchildren."

"I wish I had choices," a certain melancholy filtering into Chance's soft response.

"Everybody has or can create a choice."

"Sounds as if I could really use a wish wind."

"So could we."

＊ ＊ ＊

Wish Winds

TEN

It did not hit him just how tired he was until Saturday morning as they sat on the back porch enjoying a late breakfast. Grant tried not to think of age as an issue, but there was no doubt his stamina and alertness were now coming at a price.

They continued the discussion from dinner the night before. That day, Hattie Forester and Shelly Phelps, the two senior girls in the homeroom class had come up to his desk after the other students left and before the other senior girls arrived. Again noticing the dissimilar physical appearance, there was no denying the tears in their eyes. Between the sobs, he was able to piece together their story. Appearances aside, their friendship was the most important thing in their lives. They were constantly amazed by the similar thoughts and reactions they shared as to people and situations. They tried to do everything together and it was that togetherness that gave them great solace. Their parents thought the friendship was too close, and the girls were ordered to cut back on seeing one another and in talking so often on the telephone. Sensing how upset they were, Grant reacted as he usually did in wanting to help alleviate suffering or disappointment. He told them he would talk to their parents, and told them to tell their parents to be sure to come to the parent-teacher night scheduled in the third week of school. Without question, that effort would be a dangerous one for a new teacher at a new school, not to mention a teacher who was already controversial.

"Perhaps," Glinnis stated thoughtfully, "You should just let Dean Frentworth handle the situation as she sees fit. After all, she is the one in charge and she can counsel the parents and placate the girls."

A moment passed before Grant responded. "The girls came to me not to her. The only way I can help any of them is if they know they can come directly to me and what they tell me is strictly confidential."

"I know that. My concern is just how much responsibility you can or should handle. You are new there and you have epic struggles on that front without getting embroiled on the individual student level."

"You know who I am."

"Yes, dear. I know that very well."

"You know what I am."

"Yes, dear. I know that very well."

"So, you are just being my level-headed wife and saying what needs to be said for the record so that all of the elements are accounted for?"

"You know me very well."

"So, that part is settled. I need to do something. But, what?"

"You hopefully can get a sense of the true motive of the parents on parent-teacher night. Maybe they are merely trying to tone down the friendship so that the girls have a chance to make other friends."

"Perhaps, but it sure came across to the girls differently. If that was the desire, explaining it that way might have been more effective. I think raw feelings are at stake here."

"I just hate for you to be in the middle of a touchy situation."

His laugh was half-hearted. and spoke its own tale. "I am no stranger to difficult situations."

"I also know that very well."

"Let's change the subject and talk about something potentially more pleasant. What do you think of Chance?"

"There is a story to be told about her, that is for sure. Chance is a wonderful person with all of the right feelings and reactions. We did not run out of things to talk about, and I am certain we will be good friends. Yet, she is lonely and unhappy. It is hard for me to relate to such feelings, as I have never been either lonely or unhappy, thanks to you and the children. She never married and I think her romantic involvements have been few and far between. She alluded to two loves earlier in her life and her voice was tinged with remorse. She has started to write a novel, and that involvement may be good for her."

"Writing is a solitary experience. Sounds to me that she needs to be with people more."

"Maybe we can help her with that. Would you mind if I sacrifice some of our together time to spend it doing things with her?"

"You know I support all of your worthy causes. I could use some more nap times anyway."

"I don't think she eats well either."

"I got that impression by the meager lunches she brings to school."

"Perhaps we can have her for dinner some nights."

"That will be fine. I am sure she would enjoy looking through our books."

"Maybe we can give her a sense of family."

"Did I ever tell you that you are truly an amazing person?"

"Thousands of times."

"Did I ever tell you that I love you deeply?"

"Millions of times."

"Oh, maybe I should stop."

"Don't you dare."

✳ ✳ ✳

Wish Winds

ELEVEN

With the year-event charts blanketing the walls, the room sure looked different. The students were excited about hanging them and then reading and talking about each in detail. Everything he had hoped it would be reached total fruition. They clamored to be among the first to give the oral presentation. History had come alive in Mr. Albright's room.

There also had been little let up in the student's interest in wish winds. The allure of the unknown tinged with boundless flight of imagination, curiosity, and intrigue perpetuates involvement. He had seen it before, and it was a given that the concept would be at the forefront for the entire school year. Presenting examples of past wish winds only fueled the fire because the situations and people were so varied that the entire frame of reference took on universal characteristics. Above the blackboard he had put up a poster depicting the seeds from a dandelion blowing in the wind.

The main agitator among the faculty concerning Grant's presence and actions at the school was Phoebe Hampton, an English teacher for the past thirteen years. Her consistent complaints to Dean Frentworth and incitement of the other teachers were obvious and routinely confirmed by Melanie and Elaine who were as well considered outsiders being newcomers.

Dean Frentworth monitored one of his classes, although she did not stay long. The communication between students and teacher was so strong and so absorbing she was pleased with what she saw and heard. The students were quick to question and challenge the teacher, and the teacher thrived on the interchange and mastered the situation at each turn. In teaching as in so many other facets of life there are no better tools than maturity and experience.

It was a day that Grant and Chance were alone for lunch. Grant once again observed the scant food she was to indulge in. "I'm not as hungry as usual. Care to share this tuna salad sandwich?"

"I'm fine. Thanks for offering."

"You don't want me to tell Glinnis you turned down one of her culinary creations, do you?"

"She'll understand, I am sure. She is a very understanding person."

"That's an understatement. She has a knack for piercing barriers and fog to see what is really at stake. Many times she figures out a problem and the solution for a situation I may be wrestling with before I can even approach looking at it the correct way."

"I sense she already understands me."

"She has an added incentive to do that. She likes you."

"I like her. I like you both. I can't or don't want to get close to too many people. But you and Glinnis are real people with genuine qualities."

"We like to think so. Being that way attracts like-minded souls."

"I can see that."

"What's the story with Phoebe Hampton? She seems to have it in for me."

"I don't think she likes anyone or anything. From what I can tell she is a bitter woman. She never wanted to be a teacher. The way I hear the story, she actually wanted to be a lawyer, but her family fought her on it and there was little cooperation from society. Women still struggle in the male-dominated fields."

"And I am a prime example of a male struggling in a female dominated field."

"What we all need are the same shoes for the same feet."

"Sure would be nice, but I don't think we'll see that in our lifetime."

They were interrupted by a student entering the Library to return some books. Grant recognized the senior as Amy Weston. He had noted her petite and, there just was no other way to describe it, her frail frame. He had observed that she did not wear any lipstick or makeup as the other girls did. He had also recorded in his mind that she was among the more intelligent students because of the orderly year chart she had prepared, the concise yet detailed oral presentation, and the pointed questions she had asked at various times.

Amy placed the books on the counter and looked over at Grant. "I am glad to see you, Mr. Albright." Her voice was subdued. "I was hoping to speak with you at some time, privately."

Grant rose from the table. "That will be fine, Amy. I was just getting ready to go back to the classroom. Why don't you walk with me?"

The hallways were deserted so Amy was uninhibited in what she wanted to say. "I am very unhappy. I am not like the other girls and can't get along with them. All they want to talk about are boys, clothes, rock and roll music, and all other things I have no interest in. Their giggling drives me crazy. Can I use a wish wind to change who I am?"

Grant had an urge to hug the youngster to comfort her and convey the notion that her world was acceptable and advantageous. He squelched that impulse since he was already in enough trouble. "Amy, there is nothing wrong with you. From what I observe, you are a person with your feet firmly on the ground. It is perfectly alright not to be like others. In fact, others would probably be better off to be more like you. A wish wind is not for changing who you are but for making the most out of who you are."

It was not a smile, but her body seemed to relax. "That is nice to hear, although I am not sure I believe it. Being different is not any fun. I tried to talk to one girl I thought was understanding. I needed to tell someone about the kind of dreams I have. All she did was laugh at me. I am in all of my dreams and often there are two or three different dreams going on at the same time with totally different stories. In one way I suppose it is exciting. Yet, it is scary and reinforces the fact that I am different."

"We are all in our dreams since we are the dream makers and therefore the leading actor. What it tells you is that you have an active and probing mind with a fertile imagination. Such qualities will work well for you later in life. Now, it may all be unsettling. When it is time, a wish wind will help you to use those wonderful qualities to attain your goals. For some, happiness is not found in the present but in the future."

They reached the classroom. She ran a hand though her long and straight black hair, and for the first time looked directly at him. The glasses held up by a small nose over thin lips did not diminish the impact of wide and riveting black eyes. "I appreciate what you have said and know it is what I wanted to hear. May we talk again?"

"Sure enough."

He had checked with Chance later in the day and found out from her that Amy was a foster child who had been shunted from family to family being labeled as too somber and strange to be adopted. According to Dean Frentworth, Amy had to be pulled from the public school system because she was deemed hostile to the teachers and students. Her present foster family was wealthy enough to put her in this private school last year, but they apparently made her sign an agreement that upon graduation she would get a job and start paying them the tuition money back. There was to be no college education in Amy's future. Amy was also the most frequent user of the Library. Her classmates unkindly portrayed her as a bookworm, which they eventually shortened to just worm.

That evening he conveyed the conversation and other information to Glinnis, including his holding back on the hug. After a tender embrace, he spoke slowly. "I hate to see a troubled youngster. She cannot see or appreciate her serious nature. Growing up can be so painful. I had a student a good fifteen years ago, Evan Robertson, as you know, who also was so serious minded the other students would not accept him or adjust to him. He just did not fit in. I am sure I was of some help with the anguish. He writes occasionally, and I have shown you his flowing letters. In each letter he makes sure to thank me for being a form of bridge between his world and his peers. He is now a writer for television, mainly soap operas. He has never married and keeps saying he has yet to meet a woman with whom he can have a serious and substantial conversation. If time and space were not an obstacle, Evan and Amy might have a marriage made in Heaven, just ours is."

Glinnis sensed the torment that Grant had absorbed on behalf of Amy. That sensitivity had to be a major factor in the fervent love she had for him. He shared it with her and she gave back connecting with him emotionally as she held him close. She hoped he would not be totally drained by the end of the school year. She made up her mind to urge him to finally retire by then.

After a few quiet moments, she whispered, "Since I'll be at the school tomorrow, I would like to meet Amy."

"I thought you would. I will send her to the library to get a book for me."

"I like it best when we meet challenges together."

"I like it best when we overcome challenges together."

* * *

Wish Winds

TWELVE

From Grant's description, Glinnis was sure it was Amy who entered the Library. Keeping the harrowing thought to herself that Amy was not skinny, as Grant had portrayed, she was practically emaciated. The school uniform hung loosely over a slim frame as if it was not the proper size for her. Glinnis did not know what to do first as she had equal urges to hug her and feed her. "You must be Amy. I am Mrs. Albright. My husband told me in confidence your conversation and he wanted to give you a hug for reassurance but thought it would appear inappropriate if others saw it. I am not so restricted." She hugged that ultra thin frame and felt the small arms enfold her. There was a slight trembling in Amy's body. Glinnis was not sure if it was from apprehension or contentment.

When they broke apart, Amy stammered, "Thank you, Mrs. Albright. I don't get many hugs."

Glinnis smiled. "Hugging is a wonderful human gesture. People should hug more often. I understand you like to read."

"Every chance I get. Books are a safe place."

Glinnis read more in that remark than Amy may have intended. "Books are a doorway to the world. I have the book set aside for Mr. Albright. Please come back at the end of your lunch hour and we can search together for some books you might especially enjoy."

"I will. I would like that."

Glinnis hugged her again and watched Amy leave. Her heart went with her. There are just some people that you can sense their pain and it makes you want to relieve them of much of it as you can. It is more than empathy. It is a driving desire to help. She knew that Grant would be a participant in anything they might be able to do for Amy just as with Chance.

There was another hug for Amy when she returned at midday. Glinnis had been tempted to pull some books for her, but it would be more meaningful if they browsed through the shelves together. The more they walked, the more talkative Amy became. She was a delightful child, and Glinnis hung on every word and thought that Amy uttered. For a youngster she was eloquent both in expression and content, and her speech was tinged with just the right degree of animation to keep Glinnis spellbound. Amy's interest was broad and varied, and it was easy to tempt her to the classical literature that Glinnis had so enjoyed when she was Amy's age.

Amy eagerly nibbled at the pumpkin cupcake Glinnis had given her from the prior day's baking activity. She had brought two, one was for Chance and she was going to eat the other one until she noted Amy's physical state and saved it for her. She made a mental note to bring some treat each time she came to the school. Somehow she would put some fat on that scrawny body. It can be amazing how many missions life can present for a concerned person. Missions come in large and small degrees, but their importance is not necessarily measured by size.

Amy still had the sensation of Mrs. Albright's arms around her, and the warm feeling was highly comforting. She knew she was bitter about life and people, and that made her keenly suspicious of the motives and actions of others. Yet, the Albrights seemed different, and perhaps for the first time in her life she felt like trusting someone else. She did not have much to show for her life so far, and the future looked dismal. She desperately wanted to believe in wish winds. The other girls may not have fully grasped what this teacher was doing, but she figured it out right away and admired him for it. Believing in wish winds was just a ploy to believing in yourself. Yet, for Amy at least, that was easier said than done.

Back in Mr. Albright's class, Amy's mind wandered. She knew

it did no good to dwell on the past, but much of her awkwardness, emotional insecurity, and even lack of appetite was due to her fragmented life. She had been in more foster homes than she could remember. For the most part it had been a mere existence with an absence of affection and confidence building. She was sure the families were more interested in the money received for foster care than in her well being. It was easy to be rebellious, and it did little good to tell herself that any such actions were making a bad situation even worse. Now, on top of everything else she would have to pay the tuition moneys back to the present foster parents. It seemed like a daunting task. Would she ever have a true family? Would she ever have a girl friend? Having a boy friend appeared so remote it would be impossible, even for a wish wind.

She gulped down whatever cafeteria food she could tolerate and headed for the library. A mutual hug was an act so natural she did not think about doing it, and the warm sensation lingered.

Glinnis lead Amy slowly through the rows of bookshelves, and they stopped at one of Amy's favorite sections on poetry. This was a familiar and enchanting intellectual arena for Glinnis since she was a youngster. They took several books down, leafing through the pages and discussing the contents. They settled on an anthology of poems and Amy checked it out to be taken home. She looked forward to reading it and talking about it with Mrs. Albright. It was an exciting moment for her to have the prospect of having someone to talk to and share reactions with.

Over dinner, Glinnis described in detail her actions with Amy and her feelings of tenderness towards the youngster. She told Grant that she had already decided to give up volunteering at the University Library and at the hospital so she could be at the school three or four days a week. Chance and Amy needed her. Grant had already concluded that Glinnis needed them as well.

* * *

THIRTEEN

It was Thursday night when Chance came over for her first dinner with the Albrights. As they had guessed, she was most impressed by the books they had collected. There was a degree of melancholy as Chance looked at all of the photographs on the walls, shelves, and tables of the children and grandchildren. She was certain she would have been a good mother if she had children of her own. It was not meant to be, but she did think about it fairly often. It was one more event falling into the great unknown.

The dinner was a feast by Chance's standards, and it amazed her how simple foods can be so delicious and presented well. She admired Glinnis and could not deny that she was envious of her as well. Perhaps her old age would be enhanced by the experience of association with these new friends.

The unrestrained conversation was intelligent and witty. They tried not to talk about matters relating to the school, but talking about Phoebe Hampton and then Amy were pervasive matters. Phoebe had been secretive of late and since Chance was marked as a friend of Grant she was outside the communication network. The guess was that she was up to some adverse action, perhaps geared toward the teacher-parent night.

Each had an outpouring of emotion about Amy. Chance had been receptive to Amy's constant display of the love for books and respected her budding intelligence. Grant and Glinnis had been exposed to too many unfortunate youngsters over the years not to be drawn to one who was starved for attention and affection. The substance of childhood is crucial for what sort of adult eventually emerges, not to mention the value and enjoyment of those growing years. Once those years are gone, they can never be relived.

Glinnis packaged the leftovers for Chance to take home, except for a slice of the apple cake she had made for dessert. That piece would be for Amy.

After Chance left and the dishes were washed and put away, Glinnis curled up next to Grant on the sofa as Shostakovich's Fifth Symphony played in the background. They read for awhile, content with the warm closeness. These moments were always special as they were keen reminders of their loving past and a form of expectancy for the meaningful moments yet to come.

Chance had trouble sleeping. Her emotions were sharp and mixed. Coming from a warm and loving situation, she felt a basic contentment. Yet, there was a certain degree of depression as she reviewed that she had missed that kind of life. How different would it be if she had a husband, children, and a home she was proud of? The emptiness of her life closed in on her. As she traveled down life's winding road, who would be there for her? Glinnis and Grant might care, but she expected that they would move after this year, probably to be close to their children. There was no real purpose for them to stay. There was no real reason for her to feel sorry for herself. Yet, she cried herself to sleep.

By the next morning, Chance felt better. Crying was a crucial emotional release, and she had renewed acceptance of her abject life. At the very least, she would enjoy the fruits of friendship so long denied to her.

Amy gobbled down the cake right in front of Glinnis, and it sure was delicious. Glinnis accepted the obvious enjoyment as a compliment to her culinary endeavor. They sat together at one of the Library tables at the end of Amy's lunch break. Amy read aloud a poem that she had been especially taken with in the book she had taken home. It was by the English poet Sir Philip Sidney from the Sixteenth Century.

My True-Love Hath My Heart

My true-love hath my heart, and I have his,
By just exchange one for another given;
I hold his dear, and mine he cannot miss,
There never was a better bargain in drive;
    My true-love hath my heart, and I have his.

His heart in me keeps him and me in one,
My heart in him, his thoughts and senses guides;
He loves my heart, for once it was his own,
I cherish his because in me it bides;
    My true-love hath my heart, and I have his.

The sparkle in Amy's eyes told Glinnis how much she wanted and needed the ensuing discussion on what the poem meant. It brought back the many similar discussions she had with her children as they were introduced to the joy of reading and the intriguing thoughts to be found in literature.

Glinnis spoke slowly. "That is a beautiful sonnet. I am quite familiar with it, and I do believe we have the same taste in poetry. Actually, I recited it to Mr. Albright on our first wedding anniversary. Our hearts are full and interchangeable. Romantic thoughts and feelings can be captured in enticing ways in poetry, and that beauty is ageless."

Amy raised an eyebrow. "I can only guess what romantic is. I suppose it is a feeling in the heart."

"It is not limited to the heart. The mind can play a large part in it as well. All of the body can be consumed. Humans are at their best when they love one another."

Amy's voice sounded distant. "Love is only a word to me."

"Ah, a wonderful discovery awaits you."

"I am not sure I will find it."

"If you do not find it, it will find you."

Amy was quiet for a moment. "Do you know much about dreams?"

"I'm no expert, but have had a few in my time." Glinnis remembered Grant had said Amy was preoccupied with dreams and frustrated in not having anyone to talk to about them.

"I have very vivid dreams."

"I wouldn't doubt that considering the stress you are under. Dreams, just as crying and laughing, are probably forms of release for the mind."

"Mr. Albright says I am the dream maker so that explains why I am in my dreams. Yet, at times I am not who I am now. Sometimes, I am a small child and at other times quite old."

"Me, too."

"Really?"

"Yes. You are who you are, what you were, and what your imagination projects for what you will be."

"Do you know what a wish wind is?"

"Of course, Mr. Albright is my wish wind."

"Can a wish wind be like a dream?"

"It certainly can be, and it can be so much more."

"Will you be my wish wind?"

Glinnis hugged the frail frame close to her and held it as she spoke nearly in a whisper, "I already am."

FOURTEEN

Phoebe Hampton's scheme became clear the evening of the teacher-parent event. On a table by the front door to the school were two petitions. Both called for the removal of Grant Albright as a teacher at the school. One was signed by a majority of the existing faculty members. Phoebe beseeched the parents as they entered the building to sign the other one. By the time Dean Frentworth found out about and directed the petitions be removed, the damage had been done.

Parents first went to the auditorium for welcoming remarks by Dean Frentworth and introduction of the faculty. They were then to be encouraged to visit with the teachers in the classrooms.

The words Dean Frentworth uttered were not those she had intended. "This nation is emerging from a period of great dissent. This country is now different and probably will never be the same. Maybe that is not a bad thing. If educational institutions do not change with the times, they will be left behind in the dust. The governing Board decided that a gap existed here not only academically but also as an exposure in a limited way to the male influence and presence in the world. We hired a male teacher, coaxing him out of retirement, beloved by hundreds of students, male and female. He is here not to change anything but merely to supply an additional element so that the school can adjust to the changing times. Our girls have wasted no time or energy in accepting him. I implore you to do the same."

After recitation of the names of the old faculty, the new members were introduced individually to polite applause. Silence greeted the announcement of Grant Albright. Grant's necktie seemed tighter than he made it while dressing.

The only parents that came to see him in the classroom were Mr. and Mrs. Forester and Mrs. Phelps. Mr. Phelps had to work late that night.

Grant made a small circle with the students' desks so they could face one another. He addressed them as directly and politely as possible. "Thank you for coming tonight. There are issues far more important and personal to you than whether a male teaches here. I am not only a teacher. I am also a parent who has raised three children. Being a teacher is an easy job compared to being a parent. I do not wish to tell you how to raise your children or what your home life should be like. What I do want to tell you is what I have seen in over thirty years as a teacher and over forty years as a parent. We have a tendency to overlook the fact that it is very difficult to be a child, and the growing years are awkward and confusing. Hattie and Shelly are friends, very good friends. Having a very good friend is one of life's little blessings. Try to remember back to your school days and how comforting and supporting it was to have a good friend to share the ups and downs. It eases the way to accepting the uncertainties and the often troubling surroundings. Taking that away from them could be quite damaging."

Mr. Forester interrupted him. "Don't you think a friendship to the exclusion of other girls can also be damaging?"

"Possibly, but that is not the case here. They freely interact with others, and their shared experiences enhances what they learn and what they do."

Mrs. Phelps interjected, "I feel shut out from Shelly's life. All she talks about is Hattie this and Hattie that."

"Of course their frame of reference is formed to what is closest to them in age and the major preoccupation of their day here at school. That common bond is strong. Not talking about you or your home does not mean such are not important. In fact, that residual strength and support is often taken for granted. You and the home life will be the extended constant in their lives. The friendship, as dear as it is to them right now, may easily change over time, particularly if they go to different colleges. Right now it is a necessary crutch as they hobble along in a world they know is there but are just starting to grasp it. I don't mean to preach, but it is important not to take away the things they need and understand."

Mrs. Forester, a strikingly beautiful woman dressed immaculately so that Grant guessed she had a career of her own, spoke eloquently. "We do not want to appear unreasonable, and as you say things may change, but we have heard some terrible stories about friends who are too close."

Grant was quick to respond. "For every bad situation there is a good one. Every person is different, and so every friendship is different. What may happen to others may not happen here."

Mrs. Forester continued, "We may have been too hasty in our decision. I take to heart what you say, and I am impressed that the girls have turned to you to plead their case. It does show they have not turned their back completely on adult opinion."

"They are very upset. Youngsters need justification for authority. If it is weak they can easily rebel."

"I think I speak for us all. We will talk to the girls more about this."

Grant was pleased with how it went, particularly how these parents were so reasonable compared to the earlier events. Phoebe must be gloating.

At home, Glinnis hugged him close after he recited the evening's occurrences. "Dear, perhaps we should give this up before it takes even more out of you. At our age and place in life we need not do battle with enemies, real or imaginary."

"You are a magnificent person, and I love you even more, if that is possible, for wanting to protect me. Yet, I cannot give Phoebe the satisfaction or quit in the middle of what we chose to do."

"I should know that."

"You should also know that I will win in the end."

"Not alone you won't."

"With you, I am never alone."

FIFTEEN

The next morning, a notice in Grant's school mailbox indicated there would be a faculty meeting at the end of the day. That promised to be interesting.

Hattie and Shelly were waiting by the desk when he entered the classroom. Their arms were draped around each other's shoulders and the broad grins on their faces told it all.

"You are a miracle maker, Mr. Albright," Shelly exclaimed.

Hattie chimed in, ""They were surprisingly nice in changing their minds. My mom could not stop raving about you, and even said she wished she had a teacher like you when she was young."

Grant smiled. "As you will learn, I hope, there are times when there is more value in an idea by just saying it out loud because an idea in the open can be dealt with."

Hattie's humor defied her impulse to be quiet. "I'm not sure I understand that or ever will. But, you must have said something awfully powerful for them to come around. Thank you forever, Mr. Albright."

By the middle of the day, the entire school knew about what became known as the Hattie-Shelly victory. The students looked at him with added respect, and he imagined that Phoebe was in her chair squirming.

At the end of the afternoon homeroom, sixth grader, Tiffany Hodges, held back after the others left and approached Grant at the front of the room. Grant thought to himself, *Looks as if I will be late for the meeting.*

Tiffany was tentative in her speech. "I am hoping you can help me."

He motioned for her to sit in the front row and he sat next to her. "I will certainly try."

With her gaze directed to the floor, the hesitancy in her voice was pronounced, "I am extremely self-conscious, so much so that it makes me sick most of the time. Even the school uniform cannot hide that I have an enormous rear end. The other girls constantly make fun of me. They call me butt-head."

Once again, Grant felt the agonizing pain of those growing up. "Tiffany, what you need to do is to go stand on a busy street corner. Just as with snowflakes, no two people are the same. You will see people with heads too large or too small for their bodies, protruding ears, extra small or large noses and even crooked ones, thin and fat bodies, pinched lips, pointed chins, some too tall and some too short, as well a whole assortment of differences. Any difference, by the way, can actually be a distinction rather than a difference and needs to be looked at and evaluated with the whole picture of the person. I look at you, and I see a beautiful young woman. Your hair is full and a magnificent auburn color. Your complexion is so clear as to be out of a cosmetics catalogue. Other girls who wrestle with acne would give anything to have your skin. You have long, slender fingers. I bet you are a musician."

"I play the violin."

"People who are not musically inclined would be envious of that kind of talent. Nobody, not even me is perfect. There is a story of a young girl who thinks she is very ugly. One day, she gets on a bus and sees another young girl sitting in a row down the aisle. She thinks that girl, with flowing blonde hair and dazzling blue eyes, is the prettiest girl she has ever seen. She secretly wishes she were that girl. At the next stop that girl starts to get off. She reaches for crutches, and as she gets in the aisle the girl sees that she has only one leg."

When Tiffany smiled, Grant added, "And you have a wonderful smile."

"Thank you, Mr. Albright. You are a wish wind, for sure!"

Grant apologized for being late, but the meeting had not yet begun anyway. Melanie, Elaine, and Chance were the only ones that waved to him.

Dean Frentworth was stern looking. She cleared her throat before speaking. "I won't keep you long. This meeting should never have been necessary. That petition fiasco was embarrassing to the school and me. You have enough to be concerned about with your individual roles here and your own classes. What is best for the school is not your choice. I am placing the petition on the table before me. There is a pen beside it. I expect each of you that signed it to come up and cross off your name and initial that in the margin. Those who do not do so can expect that their contract for next year will not be renewed."

At times, short speeches can carry a large impact. All eyes turned toward Phoebe. She twisted in her seat before standing up rigidly and exiting the room. The other teachers who signed the document came up and crossed off their names.

As the meeting ended, nobody spoke. Chance whispered to Grant after most of the others had left, "If she knows she is not coming back, she'll be up to even more mischief."

✳ ✳ ✳

Wish Winds

SIXTEEN

Since he had anticipated it, it was not what she said that took Grant by surprise; it was when Glinnis said it. They had just gotten into bed and she was holding him from behind. His eyes popped open. "I think we should adopt Amy."

He turned towards her. "You've been reading my mind again. I thought the actual idea be said by you first as it might be more of a demand on you than me."

"I don't see it as a demand in any shape or manner. She is a sweetheart and has great potential, which we can help her achieve. I have to feed you anyway so I can fatten her up at the same time."

"Two old do-gooders. Maybe they won't let people of our age adopt."

"A baby, perhaps."

"We can find out. I'll call tomorrow. We should ask Amy first if she would entertain the idea."

"Does an Eskimo like snow?"

"Not a Florida Eskimo."

"Ha. Hopefully, we can get it done so we can take her with us at Christmas to meet the family when we go to California."

"A new sister and aunt will be quite a Christmas present."

" Not as much as the present life gave to me in you. I love you very much."

They kissed, a kiss that never seemed to grow old as their love took on fresh meaning with each passing day and mutual decision. When the kiss ended, Glinnis stroked his cheek. "I will talk to Amy tomorrow.

We have the spare bedroom, and Wilma had told me early on about this great used furniture store where we can hopefully find a bed, dresser, and desk. Amy can decorate the room as she would like to."

Glinnis mentioned it to Chance before she talked to Amy. Chance thought it was a wonderful idea, and she was sorry that single women could not adopt a child.

Amy was speechless. She hugged Glinnis fully intending to never let go. The simplest of gestures can have the deepest of meanings.

The procedure with the authorities went smoothly enough. The only hitch was getting the present foster parents to sign a release. The offer to reimburse them for tuition payments made and an extra thousand dollars eased the way with that.

The news of the Albrights adopting Amy spread through the school even faster than the Mattie-Shelly victory. The thought probably filtered through more than one of the girls that it was too bad they were not adoptable. In the short time Mr. Albright was revered and the students who had been in contact with her admired Mrs. Albright.

Phoebe was sure that this was just a clever maneuver by Grant to entrench himself at the school. Dean Frentworth thought it to be a noble deed, but she decided it best not to say anything about the matter since it was personal. She did believe that the year was already proving to be a very interesting one.

When they brought Amy over to see the house and her room, she was thrilled beyond words. It had to be a wish wind that carried her to a place once believed to be unattainable. A permanent home with a loving family was her fondest dream. All she could do was to hug them. She vowed to herself that she would never disappoint them or ever give them any reason to regret taking her in. It seemed beyond comprehension that two people she had really just met could do this for her. But, she had the belief that Mr. and Mrs. Albright were not ordinary people. That had to be a reflection on her as well. She would no longer consider herself as ordinary.

SEVENTEEN

Grant stood before the homeroom class gazing from one fresh face to another. "You all must be tired of talking about wish winds, so today I will read to you a very wise poem."

A voice from the back of the class brought laughter from the others. "We can talk about wish winds until the cows come home, but let's hear the poem anyway."

TRY AGAIN

Tis a lesson you should heed,
    Try, try, try again;
If at first you don't succeed,
    Try, try, try again.

Once or twice though you should fail,
    Try again,
If you would at last prevail,
    Try again.
If we strive, 'tis no disgrace
    Though we may not win the race;
What should you do in that case?
    Try again.

If you find your task is hard,

Try again;
Time will bring you your reward,
Try again.
All that other folks can do,
With your patience should not you?
Only keep the rule in view —
Try again.

The room was so quiet one could hear a proverbial pin drop. He continued, knowing full well the students would think about this realistic lesson. "There are probably times you can think of when you have given up too soon. If you had only stuck with it, success might have come after awhile. A Chinese proverb indicates that failure is not falling down but failing to get up. At times, when we fail we blame others for the failure. Yet, it is important to look at yourself because usually the lack of success is with you, the main character. Try it again, perhaps in a different way. Think about it and ask yourself what you are overlooking or discover a new approach. If it is worth doing, it is worth doing well. Probably the only real failure in life is the failure to try and try again. Maybe, Benjamin Franklin said it best: *I didn't fail the test, I just found 100 ways to do it wrong.*"

At the end of the senior class, Geraldine Hochster waited until the others had exited the room and then approached him at the desk. Tall and lanky with high cheekbones, Geraldine's voice was raspy. "Mr. Albright, I need your help as a problem solver."

"Geraldine, I am not sure I deserve that kind of credit. There are problems I cannot solve and realistically should never even attempt to solve. But, if something is troubling you, I sure will listen."

"My problem is probably not unique, so with your experience it may not be hard. I just don't know what to do."

"Let's find out. Spill it out."

"My parents insist that I go to college. I have never liked school, and dread going to college. My grades, as you probably know, show my lack of enthusiasm for studying. There is probably some college somewhere that would take me anyway."

"What do you want to do if you don't go to college?"

"I'll find a job."

"What kind of work interests you?"

"I don't know."

"You are not the first student to have come to me with this sort of difficult decision. I am sure you will not be the last. It is not unusual to doubt yourself. As with so many who have unexplored decisions ahead, it can be overwhelming. As with any tough decision, it is advantageous to look at the pros and cons. If you don't go to college, it may not be easy to find a job that interests you or even pays enough for you to not live at home. The reality is that a college education brings a higher income. It also allows time for you to settle on all kinds of decisions. The workplace itself can be as difficult to adapt to as school. The work can be boring and unsatisfying. You may have to deal with a stern and unfair boss as well as unfriendly coworkers. It may take a long time to find a work situation that you can comfortably fit in to. College, on the other hand, is unlike high school. Usually, after the first year of required courses, you may have an idea what interests you the most and what you want to major in. Then you can take some elective courses, courses you want to take, towards that end. To fully satisfy yourself, as well as ease the way with your parents, maybe it is a good idea to try that first year and see how it goes. Certainly, if at that point, you still feel this way about school, you will have a stronger case to take to your parents since you tried it their way."

Geraldine looked out of the window as if an answer was lurking out there. "I don't know. It sounds as if I can lose either way."

"At times, you don't know if you lose except when you don't win."

"You have given me much to think about. Would it be alright if we talk again?"

"Sure. If you decide to work instead, you can always go to

college later on if your parents are still willing to pay for it. Either way, nothing is set in cement. It may just prove to be a smoother choice if you try college first."

"Thank you."

Grant watched her walk away, and he was sure that part of her problem was a lack of self-confidence. That is the vital job of a parent. He recalled a very prophetic saying: *The most important things a parent can give a child are roots and wings.*

EIGHTEEN

It was a whole new world for Amy. Just having her own bedroom was a luxury. On top of that, to have a library right in the house was an exciting adventure. Wonderful meals shared with intelligent people and conversation to provoke thoughts and reactions was a new and vibrant experience. Now, it was an integral part of her surroundings.

They purchased another season pass for Amy so she could go with them to the concerts and plays. She was enthralled. There were so many facets of life and living that she never really knew existed. It was almost as if she were to go to sleep at night she would be missing out on some absorbing feature and it might not come along again.

Besides the wonderful meals and the animated conversation at the table, Amy was encouraged to go to the refrigerator whenever she wanted to. That is a rewarding feature for any teenager.

Glinnis took her clothes shopping so there would be additions to the meager wardrobe. There could now be a choice of what to wear whenever they went to the concerts, plays, and other outings. Amy especially liked the luxurious feeling of the fleece pajamas she wore around the house. Glinnis changed into pajamas shortly after dinner whenever she could, and Amy adapted to that routine rather easily. It was a fun idea. Thinking all along what a magical feeling it would be to be loved, now that she had that her newest revelation was that it was equally as wonderful to love. She loved the Albrights and considered them her real mother and father. She had the warmest of sensations that life was complete for her. Yet, the exhilaration kept growing because she believed there would actually be more to come.

Amy took great pride in her room, especially the coverlet that Glinnis had let her pick out at the store. So far, the only wall decoration was the same poster that Grant had in the classroom of the dandelion seeds being blown in the wind. Grant, at her request, was able to find another one. He would have thought she would want a poster of a rock and roll star, but Amy's maturity ran in a different direction than popular personalities or current fads. The dandelion poster was a constant reminder that her wish wind had been fully realized.

At the school, Grant wanted to give the fourth graders the opportunity to make charts to be hung on the walls. As an offshoot from the penny assignment, he let the students pick a postage stamp from a bowl filled with stamps. Each of the stamps was dedicated to a famous person, and the students were to do a chart and give an oral presentation on that selected person. The girls thought this a delightful idea.

It became known that Phoebe capitulated and crossed off her name from the petition. Even small victories can bring substantial satisfaction.

Now that Glinnis went to school each day, they would drop Amy off at the front door to the school before they proceeded to the faculty parking. Even the car trips were considered family time. Amy was so animated as a result of her happiness, in the car she would often bubble forth with ideas she read or developed on her own. A young and happy mind knows no bounds. Grant and Glinnis would glance over to the other, a knowing smile crossing their lips. Amy called them mom and dad, and she giggled loudly the first time she heard them refer to each other as momma bear and poppa bear. Amy was bombarded by questions by the other girls on what it was like to be living with the Albrights. She did not have to invent stories as the truth erupted in colorful descriptions. Even her dreams were a reflection of her new posture and were calmer and far less upsetting.

The telephone calls from their own children were more frequent now as they were curious about the new family member. They had taken the news in stride, knowing full well that their parents were truly concerned about troubled youngsters. They had lived with that all of their growing years, and they were proud of their parents. They were confident that such a trait, as well as the many others they admired, would rub off on them. In fact, the greatest surprise about Amy's adoption was that such a step had not been taken numerous times in the past when it would have been beneficial to a child. They concluded that Amy must be very special, and they looked forward to officially welcoming her to the family.

A few days later, Chance came over for dinner, and she sensed the family closeness. Amy was helpful and stared at the Albrights as if she took her eyes off of them they might disappear. It made Chance wonder again what she may have missed not having children. All of this inspired her more to work on the book. She had tried Glinnis' suggestion of playing music in the background. While that did not lead to more writing, it did help to fill up the many moments that her mind wandered. It was as if she needed to live the friendship to its fullest extent before she could write about it. That seemed to be logical as well as the most satisfying approach. No doubt the actual experience would enrich the writing. Hope takes many varied forms and has many different outcomes. Perhaps, that is why hope is truly magical.

✳ ✳ ✳

Wish Winds

NINETEEN

Not having fourth graders before, it came as a bit of a surprise to discover that such youngsters could also have problems looming monumental to them. Kaleen Hopper, a quiet and shy youngster, who never raised her hand, held back to talk to him as the other fourth graders cleared the room. As soon as her timid voice sounded, he realized that she had a slight stutter. Freckles adorned a round face on a thin body. Long eyelashes emanated over deep brown eyes matching long straight dark brown hair.

He took off his glasses and cleaned the lenses with his handkerchief. "The clearer I can see you, the better I will be able to hear you."

A partial smile accentuated the slight quivering of her lower lip. "I know you said a wish wind is for us alone, but I need a wish wind for my mother."

"She can have her own wish wind."

"I don't think she knows how and I don't know enough about it to show her."

"Tell me what it is all about."

A sigh preceded the account, the stuttering becoming more pronounced the more she spoke. "She pretends to me that everything is fine, but she is very sad. After I have gone to bed, I can hear her crying. She tries to hide it. I know, and I lay there sometimes for a long time listening to her."

Grant took his glasses off again as he noted the tears in her eyes. "Maybe there is a way to bend a wish wind to help. Do you know why she is so unhappy?"

"No."

"Where is your father?"

"They are divorced. He is supposed to see me every other weekend, although it is more like once a month, if at all."

"Does that bother you?"

"Not really. He wasn't around much, and I think he only paid attention to me because I was there."

Here was another instance where he wanted to hug the child so she would know that she was not alone. No child should have to endure less than a full life. It was not only the mother that was unhappy. "Do you think your mother is unhappy because of the divorce?"

"Maybe, but she was unhappy even when they were married."

"I will tell you a secret about wish winds. You cannot let another have your wish wind, but you can have a wish wind that helps others."

"How does that happen?"

You can have a wish that your mother will feel better. The wind can move you to help. Talk to your mother and tell her you know she is unhappy. Tell her you want to help her in anyway you can, even if she wants to express to you her thoughts and feelings so things are not bottled up inside of her. Offer to help with chores around the house, with food shopping, or anything else to ease her way. Suggest a mother-daughter outing, such as going to the movies, or to have a meal at a restaurant. Just let her know that you are there for her. She will appreciate that you are not only her daughter but also her friend. That alone may well lift her spirits. I have learned over my long years that any unhappiness becomes less troublesome when it is shared with another. Maybe, just by her knowing that you know so she does not have to hide it from you may be a great relief for her."

"I just knew you could help me. I want you to be my teacher forever."

"Now, that is a tall order."

"You know what I mean."

"Yes, I do. Please let me know how you make out."

On the way home, Grant related the story about Kaleen. Glinnis and Amy expressed approval on what he said. Amy indicated she would pay some special attention to Kaleen. Grant was not only her new father; he was also her hero. His mission to help others was now her cause as well. She would become a wish wind maker.

* * *

TWENTY

Grant allotted some time after dinner most days to read mail from former students. Many did not have his new address and there was often a delay in the post office forwarding them. Few prompted a response as they were generally reporting on news of accomplishments attributed in part to the intellectual and emotional foundation he had established in their lives. Former students took pride laying out the fruits of his teaching and guidance. As a teacher it was heartwarming to read these recitals. As a human being, he felt elated that these people had reached contentment and useful mileposts on the highway of life.

At rare times, he was moved to write a response. Few letters actually requested a reply. It was the letters where he sensed a need to reinforce, clarify, or complete a lesson learned or an idea or dream still unfulfilled that inspired him to respond. On rare occasions it was when a wish wind had been abandoned.

Nelson Zeller was a student of his for the years 1955 to 1957. Nelson knew from the very start that Mr. Albright was different from other teachers and it did not take long for him to consider him as his idol. Mr. Albright shunned the staid and time ensconced system of seating students alphabetically. Mr. Albright would sit the students based on all sorts of factors, particularly as to size so that there would be ease in seeing the blackboard. Some he would just invite to sit wherever they would like to. When he saw that Nelson's last name started with the last letter in the alphabet, he pointed to a seat in the front row right between the two prettiest girls in the school.

Nelson was now an attorney in a small law firm in New York

City, and he prided himself in handling cases in what others would call unpopular causes even if the clients could not pay. He found that fulfilling, and he attributed this unusual passion to Mr. Albright who espoused time and time again that some people deserve special attention because of individual circumstances or because of societal treatment. His letters, maybe once a year, were usually about a particular case he handled in which he thought he made a difference. This letter was different.

Dear Mr. Albright,

During a recent unusual quiet period, I remembered a talk we had after class one day. You had talked in class about turning points in the lives of people, a time or an event if it had been handled differently could have altered the course of that life. I had stayed after class to ask you how I might recognize such a turning point in my own life when it should happen. You had said it might be years later when it might become clear, if ever. As with all of the ideas you presented, I made it a part of who I am, although I must admit that at the time I had doubts about the concept ever applying to me.

I am satisfied with my professional accomplishments. It has been my personal happiness that I have been grappling with. I had been shy and inexperienced in dealing with people's feelings, especially my own. Before your class, I viewed the learning process from the back of the classrooms, and I struggled with an overly protective mother.

In my first class with you, you sat me next to Lindsey Crawford, one of the prettiest girls in town. I had worshipped her since the third grade, and I don't think she knew I was alive. I finally was able to get enough courage to speak to her being so close, and in our senior year we dated. We went to the same college and became sweethearts. Despite knowing the importance of that relationship to my happiness, my all-consuming immaturity prevented me from protecting and nourishing that relationship until, finally, in exasperation she broke off with me. I did not handle the situation well from start to finish. If I had been more mature, all might have been different. In a recent re-examination of my life, I have found the turning point.

The summer before my high school senior year, my parents sent me to a children's camp in the Adirondacks. I was old enough to be a waiter in the dining room, but my mother did not want me to do that kind of work thinking I was not up to it physically. So, I was put in the older boys group of which I was the oldest and thus restricted as a camper whereas the waiters had a great deal of freedom, especially with the girls. I believe that was my turning point. In the atmosphere of the camp, akin to a small town life, I was set back emotionally. If I were a waiter, I believe my maturity would have been advanced. I would have been a year ahead instead of held back. I am firmly convinced that year's potential "growth" was crucial.

I have never married, and have never felt as strongly with any female as I did with Lindsey. Dating has been awkward and unfulfilling. Other than as an academic exercise, it does little good to discover an earlier turning point. Wouldn't it be more advantageous to know the turning point when it happens so we can do or not do for our own good?

Forgive my rambling. Of all the people I have ever come across in this life, I know you are the one person I feel unrestrained in what I say. I just know you understand what I am about.

Nelson

It had taken three weeks for the letter to be forwarded, and Grant was moved to respond right away as Nelson was undoubtedly hoping for a word from his teacher. He gave the letter to Glinnis to read, and her response was as he expected. "The poor fellow is beating up on himself."

Dear Nelson:

I just received your letter since I had moved and it needed to be forwarded. See the return address on the envelope. I came out of retirement to be the token male at an all girl's school, and that has proven to be somewhat of an unpopular and combative cause. It may well be a turning point for me.

I sense your pain in a regret that you have attributed to a turning point in your life. When and how one attains a mature demeanor and able to use such to foster goals is probably not a true turning point. Maturity is merely a tool to accomplish rational action. It is unlikely that it is the sole factor in the failure of a love relationship. Besides there being another person in the equation, so many other factors can enter the picture.

As an old man sees it, the secret to happiness is not to dwell on the past and what may or may not have been a turning point but to use that hindsight as a lesson in moving forward. A loving relationship will come along and the most important thing for you to do is to be prepared to recognize it free of any ghosts of the past, to meet it head on and to make the most of it. Please stop punishing yourself over an event long gone. A regret can be so counter productive.

You are helping others, but do not exclude helping yourself. More than a turning point, you need to turn the corner that looms before you in your life travels. Make that the decisive point. Deal with what greets you without looking back.

Grant Albright

He gave the response to Glinnis to read before he sealed the envelope. She hugged him as she handed it back to him. "You sure are one wise old man."

"Wise enough to know I am lucky to have a wise old lady at my side. At times I take happiness with you for granted, and I would not want to be in Nelson's shoes and have to seek for it."

"A noble wish wind would be for all people to find our kind of happiness. As exemplified by your letter you are guiding those that you can. Unfortunately, people are imperfect in an imperfect world. We see it time and time again, for so many life is a series of struggles. All you can do is to do your part.

"Don't you mean our part?"

"Of course."

* * *

TWENTY-ONE

When he would later recall it, Grant labeled it "The Pre-Thanksgiving Surprise." It was the day before the four-day Thanksgiving break. Before the homeroom class was due to enter, he had just settled in the chair behind his desk rereading a few Thanksgiving poems he was going to share with the students. He looked up over his glasses when he heard the door open. It was the last visitor he ever expected.

It took what she thought was great courage to come to talk to him. Yet, Phoebe Hampton had mustered whatever it took all her life when an unexpected or unwanted situation arose. Upon much introspection, and closely listening to the many student comments about Grant, she knew she had misjudged him and done him unnecessary harm. You would think a woman of her age and experience would look at a person for who he or she was rather than letting the situation or events dominate a conclusion. Too many in her life had caused her anguish for her not to recant an opinion after it had been established that she was wrong.

She approached the desk, and he really had no idea what to expect. "May I?" Her voice was friendly as she motioned to the chair in the front of the desk.

She sat down in response to the half smile that crossed his lips. "I owe you an apology, and I am here to pay my debt. In spite of what you may think of me as being mean and unfair, I do try to correct any wrong created by my deeds or words. Listening to the girls speak so highly of you, particularly how you have helped some of them, my first impression of you as an interloper and opportunist was wrong. I am probably not as good a judge of character as I believe I am."

Since she hesitated, he thought it best to say something as he sensed it was difficult for her to be in this position. "When you get to be my age, and you have a long way to go, you will find that at times too hasty a judgment has a knack of coming back to haunt you."

"Apparently so. I am not sure I am a good teacher or, for that matter, a good person. But, that is my cross to bear."

"The girls speak well of you as a teacher, and I can appreciate that. They do know best. As far as being a good person, that is constantly in your power to display. I appreciate your apology, and in my book only a good person can admit a mistake and express regret to those affected by it."

"And I appreciate you letting me off the hook so easily. I expected some harsh words, but I should have known better of that too."

He watched her leave, and knew it would not be until lunch before he could tell Glinnis and Chance that the iceberg had melted. That would be welcome news.

At the end of the day while Glinnis and Amy were waiting for Grant in the car, Amy had a serious look on her face. "Mom, you have helped me with my dreaming. I need your help in another area."

"Sure, sweetie, what is it?"

"I have read much in the literature about romance and romantic feelings, but I am not so sure I grasp the true meaning of it all."

"You should not be overly concerned about it. The idea takes form and shape in experience."

"What is the most romantic feeling you have with Dad?"

"That's an easy one. Sure, the first kiss and each of the later ones are memorable and sentimental, not to mention embraces and caresses. Yet, the first time he held my hand I sensed the power of love. A simple act of love can often be the deepest. Each and every time we hold hands, with fingers intertwined, it signifies the love we share."

"When you took me to meet Wilma and Benny, their sons stared at me. What is all that about?"

"Honey, that is a far cry from romantic. Teenage boys have one overriding interest and it is not romantic. They think and feel with their groins and not their hearts or minds."

Grant appeared and slipped behind the steering wheel. He smiled at the two passengers and before he put the key in the ignition he reached for and pressed Glinnis' hand firmly. Amy soaked it all in. The thought lingered in her mind as they drove home, *When is my hand-holder going to come along?*

❋ ❋ ❋

Wish Winds

TWENTY-TWO

As their children grew old enough to participate fully in holiday preparations, Glinnis let them share the special effort at making the holiday dinner table festive. She would take them into the woods to gather all sorts of natural decorations befitting the occasion. There might be colored rocks and leaves, flowers, pine cones, odd-shaped pieces of wood, and twigs that could be bent to make shapes of animals and structures. Amy excitedly fell into the enterprise, and the two of them had a grand time at the park collecting items for the Thanksgiving table.

The shopping for food was a family affair. Chance was the invited guest and offered to bring a salad. So, they only had to get the turkey, sweet potatoes, green beans, apples for Glinnis' apple pie, and the ice cream to crown the creation. Amy was a constant learner in the shopping and cooking process, and in some ways she felt that she had been in the family for a long time.

They telephoned the children out west in the middle of the day to allow for the time difference. Amy also talked to them, and animation was matched by animation. The Christmas visit was not that far off and Amy was particularly excited. Going from no family to a large one represented an amazing achievement.

For Amy and Chance, holiday feasts had been more of a concept than an event to participate in. Now, a family around the dinner table made the occasion warm and memorable.

Between the main part of the meal and the purposefully delayed serving of the pie, Grant sat in the living room in the easy chair to take a nap. Amy went to her room to read.

It was a relatively warm day, but Glinnis and Chance put on sweaters to ward off any chill before they went out on the back porch to sit in the rockers. A row of trees separated them from the houses on the street beyond, and the houses along side were not visible from the back.

After a few minutes of silence, Chance started speaking in a low and hushed voice that Glinnis could just about hear. "Normally, I don't think about death. Lately, I have started to think about it a great deal. It is said that before you die your life passes before your eyes. I see my life, what little there is of it, streak through my mind. On a day as this one when I partake in the reality of a family, I realize with a shudder of horror that I have no family. I have no one who cares about my living, so there is no one to care about my dying. No one will come to my deathbed to hold my hand or wipe my brow. That is a sadness that seeps in to my very soul and leads me to want a quick death." Her voice trailed off to a whisper and Glinnis could not catch any of the additional words or thoughts. It was almost as if she were speaking to herself all along.

Glinnis rose from the chair and hugged Chance firmly. A steady hug is designed to soothe the spirit. "My dear Chance, please consider us as your family. We love you. We care about you. We want you to know and believe that we are here for you each and every day. You have many accomplishments ahead of you. The book needs to be completed, and that is an adventure you will relish. Students at the school need your guidance for and about reading. The ones you bring to the world of reading is a major success. I need you as a dear and close friend. I consider you to be that and it is important to me. The old saying is very true. We are all angels with one wing, and we need others to fly. As I grow older, I realize how very precious life is. Each day is important and each day represents an opportunity to make ourselves and others happy." She took a deep breath and renewed the grasp of Chance's frame. "We are your family. You are loved and need not ever consider yourself alone."

Chance's voice was barely audible. "I did not mean to ruin your day."

"You have not ruined my day. Having you here has made it extra special. I am also glad to have had a reason to tell you how much we care."

"I love you, my friend."

* * *

Wish Winds

TWENTY-THREE

Standing before the homeroom class, Grant laughed loudly. The students looked at him as if he had lost his mind. "Laughing and crying are two of the greatest releases for the mind and body. From now until the Christmas break, just two weeks away," he stopped long enough to laugh again, "We will be talking about what can be one of the most delightful human characteristics, one which I am hoping each of you will develop fully if you have not done so already. I am referring to a sense of humor. The seniors in the class will need this especially since after Christmas there is the serious matter of applying to colleges. A joke or riddle are the obvious attributes of a sense of humor. Here, we will concentrate on the less obvious, the subtle aspects which by an outlook or interpretation you can turn a serious matter into a smiling response or lighten the air when a situation may be tense. It is more than using a wish wind for getting the Christmas present you want." The girls laughed and looked at one another with understanding. "At times, the funniest thing is one unintended provided you can laugh at it knowing what is said or done can have more than one meaning, one of which is humorous in nature. I remember when my children were young. We went on a car trip and came to a railroad crossing. The safety arm came down, lights flashing. When the train passed, the arm did not budge. One of my daughters blurted out, 'It is probably better to be stuck down than to be stuck up.' Of course, she meant that from a safety point-of-view it is preferable the arm be in the down position if it cannot move. With a sense of humor, it is clear that the word stuck-up, meaning conceited, makes the statement funny. It is better not to be conceited if you have a choice."

One of the girls held back after the others went off to class. Belinda Jenkins, a sixth grader, stood before him with a very serious look on her youthful face. "Mr. Albright, I am so glad you are talking about a sense of humor. I wanted to talk to you about that. I was just waiting for the right chance. I have no sense of humor at all. I find nothing funny. Others laugh at almost anything. I laugh at nothing. It even hurts to smile."

"Ah, Belinda, then you may get the most out of these sessions. Listen carefully and think about what is said."

"I will, but I don't think it will help. I can't force laughter."

"If all else fails, we'll see about performing an operation on your funny bone."

She did not even crack a smile. Grant thought to himself, "This may be tough, but I am going to get some laughter out of her eventually."

On the trip home, Grant told Glinnis and Amy about Belinda. Glinnis offered, "When you can't laugh at others, it may be best to laugh at yourself."

"What does that mean?" Amy's inquisitive mind never rested.

Glinnis turned and looked at her. "It is one of those expressions that has a double connotation. It means that to see humor elsewhere you first have to see humor within yourself, that is, to see humor you have to be humorous. It also means that since we know ourselves best, if we have to we should find something funny about ourselves."

Amy continued on the subject, "Most of the people I have known just have no appreciation of humor and are sourpusses."

"Those are the people you can feel sorry for," Grant interjected. "They miss a great deal of pleasure in appreciating the bright side in and about life."

"I hope I have a sense of humor."

"You have, sweetie," Glinnis interposed.

Grant sneered. "Hanging around us you'll get it by osmosis. We leave the serious for the serious. Everything else is fun."

Amy smiled. That is just the way she would like it to be.

* * *

TWENTY-FOUR

The next day, Fifth grader, Margaret Fieldstone, came up to speak to him when the homeroom class emptied out. Margaret was short and stocky with long red hair, freckles, and thick glasses. Her voice was squeaky, "May I ask your opinion about something, Mr. Albright?"

"Sure, Margaret."

"It is not easy to talk about."

"Most problems are that way. Take your time and just say it as you feel it."

She took a deep breath. "My parents are getting a divorce and they are fighting over custody of me. I gave you the note from the office that I won't be in tomorrow. I have to go to court. The judge is going to ask me which parent I want to live with." She grew silent and Grant noted the tears swelling in her eyes. Glasses are not only for seeing outwards they can also enable peering within. Staring deep into Grant's eyes, she continued in a strained voice. "Everyone expects me to choose my mother. Her lawyer, relatives, and others keep telling me that is the natural way it should be. I do love my mother, but I also love my dad. I am more like him, and I want to be with him. Is that so wrong?"

Grant delayed responding for a moment. "Nothing is wrong for you to express how you feel. Especially is this so if they ask you to do so. Even if you prefer to be with your father, and the judge will certainly consider your preference, there may be other factors involved. I believe a father can raise a child as well as the mother if all other matters are equal. Your father might not have a suitable place to raise you or his job may make time to be spent with you too difficult. It is just too bad you are put in the position of having to make a choice. I hope it can work out the way you want it to. They both must love you very much and, while it is hard to understand, there are times that children are better off with one parent than with two when there is an unhappy home. Above all else, Margaret, no matter what happens you must be strong for yourself."

She cast her eyes downward. "Thank you. I worry about tomorrow and the future, but I will try to be strong. I need a wish wind badly."

"If you are strong the wish wind will be there at some point."

He watched her leave, once again agonizing over a situation children must bear caused by others. There are enough setbacks in the adult world. Children should be spared from the shocks and disheartening moments at least for a time. Too many children do not have a childhood.

He was quite tired when they arrived home. There was another delayed letter to greet him that he was moved to respond to.

Dear Mr. Albright,

I would be surprised if you remember me. My name is Charles Enders. I was in the very first class you taught at the high school. I rarely participated in class, and I never had the nerve to stay late or come early to ask you about things you presented to us which really were so obvious but difficult to accept. I try to think for myself and even if I don't successfully examine a situation beforehand, I do go back numerous times in my mind to analyze the role I played.

I did not go to college and worked in my father's small packaging business. He died soon thereafter and I ran the business. It is not glamorous but it is a comfortable living. I married a woman I thought I loved and she completely deceived me as the kind of person I thought she was. Some people are truly evil. Anyway, we had two daughters who I raised myself after she left me as being too boring. They have always been wonderful. So, here is the dilemma I keep dwelling on. If you can't have a good wife and good children, is it better to have a good wife and bad children or a bad wife and good children?

The world is my classroom, and you are still my teacher. I would most appreciate your view if you have time and the inclination to respond.

Sincerely,

Charles

After she read the letter, Glinnis sighed. "I am glad I am not the teacher."

"Are you a good wife?"

"The best you'll ever have."

"Then you don't have to be the teacher."

Dear Charles,

Your letter was delayed in getting to me as the post office had to forward it to me. I am in North Carolina, coaxed out of retirement to teach at an all girls' school. It is quite a challenge, but I am enjoying it more than I thought I would. The world of young minds keeps me young.

It is usually good to think intensely about our participation in life. Yet, at times it may create a false dilemma. You have good children and that is a mighty blessing. Now, with good children and your experience meeting and marrying a bad wife just go out and find yourself a good wife. Then, you will have it all. I am convinced there are many wonderful people all around us. It just takes some effort to find and befriend them. Be attentive and receptive. And most of all, be patient.

You were in my class before I started to employ the concept of a wish wind. Set a clear goal and the wish itself will engender a wind to carry you there. When you know where you are going, it is easier to focus on the trip.

Yours truly,

Grant Albright

Glinnis read the response before he sealed the envelope. "Right on the button. But, if I extend your logic, perhaps you should be looking for a gooder wife."

"No such word and no such thing."

"Just testing you."

"Did I pass?"

"Barely." She reached for his hand. As their fingers intertwined she bent over and kissed his knuckles. Long ago her feeling towards him had surpassed love. She worshipped him.

TWENTY-FIVE

As they were finishing dinner the following evening, Amy was pensive when Glinnis asked her what she was thinking about in the way of college. Glinnis and Grant had decided earlier to raise the subject that night. They believed all things should be talked through.

College and even a future seemed so remote a short time ago that Amy was not sure her thoughts had fully formed. Blurting it out made it decisive. "I want to be a teacher!"

"Why am I not surprised?"

"If I ever can become half as good as Dad, I'll be satisfied."

Glinnis looked over at Grant and noticed the smile on the thin lips. "He has inspired many to become teachers, and while he is the best you surely can become equally as good."

"I hope so."

Grant looked at Amy and was amazed at how quickly they had accepted her and loved her. As far as he could tell, and he was a good judge, she was an exceptional person with tremendous potential.   "It seems to me there are two levels of decision-making here. I know Duke has an Education Department, but for an aspiring teacher there are many advantages to going to a small teacher's college where the program is more concentrated and all the students have a commonality. The informality leads to a quality dedication to the field and some lasting friendships. The advantage of a larger university is if you change your mind along the way it is easier to shift to another program."

Amy was emphatic. "I will not change my mind. But, I feel badly that you have to spend so much money on me. I will try to get a part-time job, and maybe I can find something for the summer."

Glinnis jumped right in, "We did it for all our other children and you are now and always will be our child. We scrimped and saved, took few vacations, and shaved expenses wherever we could. Unfortunately, teachers are paid far less than they're worth and for the responsibility they have. We got the whole gang through, although they knew they had to live at home and commute to save money."

"That is surely not a problem for me. That is where I want to be."

Glinnis smiled and hugged her. "Fortunately, we have some money from the house sale up north that we did not have to put as a down payment on this house."

Grant continued as if the intervening conversation had not taken place. "The other level of decision-making is do we stay here or move to California? I am sure there are teacher's colleges near where the families are centered."

"That's a tough decision," Amy offered. "You must decide that."

"Wrong, young lady," Grant bellowed. "It's a family decision and for good or bad you are part of the family."

Glinnis reached across the table for his hand, Amy smiling at the gesture. "What will you do if they ask you to teach again next year?"

Grant thought for a moment. "I really don't know, although I think that will not happen. After all, I am an experiment. If it is determined some male teachers would be beneficial, they can get some others, younger ones who will grow with the institution. If they think the effort is not justified, I will fall by the wayside. I am still not sure I am fully welcome there. While major adversities may be diminished, there is still an uneasy undercurrent."

Amy could not control herself. "But, you are so good. The girls think you are the best teacher there."

"Students do not make executive decisions. Besides, I retired once and the same reasons are sound now. You can love what you do but the strain does not go away."

"I am sorry," Amy gushed. "I did not mean to influence you, and I should learn to keep my mouth shut."

"Nothing is out-of-bounds in a family discussion. We'll cross bridges when we get to them. We can still live here if we find a teacher's college close by and we decide to be here for a while. I can get a job at a bakery making jelly doughnuts. I always wanted to try doing that."

Amy chuckled. "You could open a wish wind shop."

"Ah," Grant sighed, "You can't sell a wish wind. The magic of it comes from within people. I better stick to jelly doughnuts."

* * *

TWENTY-SIX

Unforeseen events can have a major impact on plans and decisions. An unexpected occurrence can cause upheavals in the lives of those directly involved as well as those who are affected by the unfolding action, in whole or in part. The upheaval can be monumental. It can be life changing.

It was two days before the Christmas break and four days before the scheduled trip to California. When Glinnis entered the library, she found Chance slumped over on the desk in her office. Checking for a pulse, as there was no telephone in the library she rushed out in the hallway and grabbed the first student who came by sending her quickly to the office to call for an ambulance immediately.

Within minutes, Dean Frentworth rushed in to the library informing Glinnis that the ambulance was on its way. Glinnis thought it best not to move Chance, but had lifted her head and placed a seat cushion under it.

Glinnis rode in the ambulance to the hospital. Dean Frentworth went to Grant's classroom to inform him of what had transpired. Since the arrival of the ambulance had stirred rumors, she went on the public address system announcing that the librarian had been taken to the hospital and that was all that was known at this time.

At the end of the day, Grant and Amy went to the hospital and found Glinnis at the bedside of a still unconscious Chance. The diagnosis was as yet incomplete, but it was determined that Chance had a stroke but its extent and prognosis had to await further tests. The doctors were not certain that she would ever gain consciousness.

Glinnis would not leave, the foretelling discussion she had with Chance at Thanksgiving fresh in her mind. If Chance were to regain consciousness, Glinnis wanted her to know she was not alone.

Grant and Amy stopped at a diner to get a bite to eat and then proceeded home. They left for school earlier than usual the next day, the last day of school before vacation time, and stopped at the hospital with fresh clothes and toiletries for Glinnis. The hospital staff had put a cot next to Chance's bed for Glinnis to get some sleep. There had been no change in Chance's condition.

Glinnis had already decided that if Chance recovered enough to leave the hospital, they would bring her home to care for her. Amy offered to sleep on the sofa so Chance could have the bedroom. Any remaining days would be surrounded by caring and love. Chance may not have had a family before, but she would have one now.

Chance died a week later never having gained consciousness. Her friend was there with her to the end. Grant finally brought an exhausted Glinnis home. They had to cancel the California trip and told the family they would make up for the visit during the spring break. Grant mailed the Christmas presents.

Dean Frentworth had been a frequent visitor to the hospital. Upon Chance's death, she asked Glinnis if she would stay on and serve as the librarian until the end of the school year as she was now familiar with its operation. They would get a new librarian next year. Glinnis agreed considering the act as a form of tribute to Chance.

A special assembly was held at the school to honor the memory of Chance. Dean Frentworth acknowledged the accomplishments of the woman who had served in the background for such a long time. Glinnis added some personal words about Chance's love for books and the library and her quest to encourage as many of the students as possible to read often.

That night as Grant held her tenderly, Glinnis sobbed for a long time. Tears shed for a friend. Even a friendship of short duration can be a powerful bond. The memory of that friendship would endure for Glinnis until her own final days.

* * *

TWENTY-SEVEN

By February, Grant was taken somewhat by surprise when Dean Frentworth extended an invitation for him to teach for another year. Glinnis was also taken aback when asked to be the school librarian for the next school year. However, the Albrights, as the result of numerous family discussions, had already made the decision to govern their future. Also, the more they talked about colleges, the more Amy was in favor of a small teacher's college. She believed she would be lost at a large school and would be more at ease in a smaller environment.

As flattering as it was to be asked to return, Grant and Glinnis, fresh from the experience and significance of Chance's death, had firmly decided they would finally retire and move to California to be with and enjoy their family. They knew it would be wonderful to be part of the growing years of the grandchildren and to share the landmarks along the way. They had already missed out on too much of that. In some small way they might even be able to contribute worthwhile content and example for the ensuing years. Added incentive was supplied by their son Corey and his plans and efforts to move closer to Hannah and Elizabeth.

The prevailing thought was that their health might turn at any point for the worse, and the most important and comforting feature would be to have their children, who were willing and able, to look after and care for them and ease the way down the final pathway. Amy repeatedly announced she would, if it came to it, give up anything in her personal life to care for them wherever they were. They loved her for that sentiment but would not want her to shoulder that burden alone.

The fruits of literature and their own experience taught them that more important then friends, familiar surroundings, and rewarding endeavors, was a loving family to be with when the point was reached when they might not be able to care for themselves or one another.

So, it was planned that when they were in California for the spring break they would look for a house and a college in the general vicinity of where the children resided. The children would do some preliminary scouting and narrow the choices.

On the final day of school, Grant lost count of how many students hugged him good-bye, exclaiming they would never have another teacher as wonderful as he had been. Even Phoebe came by to wish him well and to reiterate her apology for making things more difficult for him. Dean Frentworth thanked him profusely for leaving a mark of distinction on all of their lives.

A wish wind need not cover a singular goal. At times, various factors may form a pattern that portends a memorable tomorrow. For Grant and Glinnis a wish wind would propel them to and through the final phase of their life together. The wish wind, as it had always been, was love.

✳ ✳ ✳

Wish Winds

www.ingramcontent.com/pod-product-compliance
Lightning Source LLC
Chambersburg PA
CBHW031840170626
46807CB00004B/1555